RUNAWAY AT SEA

RUNAWAY AT SEA

by Mary Razzell

HARBOUR PUBLISHING

Published by
Harbour Publishing Co. Ltd.
P.O. Box 219, Madeira Park, BC V0N 2H0
www.harbourpublishing.com

Cover design by Anna Comfort and Roger Handling
Page layout by Anna Comfort
Cover photo of porthole copyright 2005 by Susumu Kohda/Phontonica
Cover photo of teen girl copyright MedioImages
Printed and bound in Canada

Harbour Publishing acknowledges financial support from the Government of Canada through the Book Publishing Industry Development Program and the Canada Council for the Arts, and from the Province of British Columbia through the British Columbia Arts Council and the Book Publisher's Tax Credit through the Ministry of Provincial Revenue.

The Canada Council for the Arts since 1957 | Le Conseil des Arts du Canada depuis 1957

Library and Archives Canada Cataloguing in Publication

Razzell, Mary, 1930-
Runaway at sea / Mary Razzell.

ISBN 1-55017-327-8

I. Title.

PS8585.A99R85 2005 jC813'.54 C2004-907478-4

Dedicated to the memory of Brian P. Slinn, son of Judy and Peter Slinn of Penticton, BC. Loved and missed.

Special thanks to Gordon Dixon Webb, Ph.C., M.R.P.S., of George Town, Tasmania, Australia, with gratitude for his expert help. Without it, this book could not have been written.

CHAPTER ONE

I should have known something was wrong when the hotel clerk peered over his glasses and asked, "You really sure you want to register here, Miss?"

Was sixteen too young? "What do you mean?" There was a dusty smell of old wallpaper.

"Not usually the kind of hotel for a girl like you—remind me of my own granddaughter."

"It's close to everything," I said.

"Such as?"

"The science fair."

"Ever been in 'Frisco before?"

"A few times with my family."

"They know you're here?"

"How much is it?" I dropped my backpack to the floor and looked for my wallet, which was buried under my spare socks.

"Two dollars the night."

I picked up the key he slid across the scarred counter. It felt grimy between my fingers.

"Room 202," he said. "Bathroom's down the hall."

I took the stairs to the second floor, which smelled of beer and mildew. The narrow hallway of black wood had a strip of scuffed linoleum, bottle-green, down the middle.

Room 202 itself was filled with heavy, dark furniture, and curtains hung dismally at windows too dirty to see through. But I'd only be there to sleep, and at two dollars a night—and in downtown San Francisco at that—it would do.

But I didn't sleep well. The sheets were stiff, and the blanket was too short and was soon on the floor. During the night, people tried to get in. Sometimes they knocked; sometimes they fumbled at the doorknob. Finally I got up and pushed the heavy wooden dresser in front of the door, then slept in fits and starts until about five-thirty. When I opened the closet door to get my clothes, I noticed another door inside the closet, at the far end. Opening it just a crack, I saw narrow, twisting stairs leading down.

I couldn't get out of there fast enough. I pushed the dresser back, opened the door to the hallway cautiously and fled down to the lobby.

The same clerk was on duty, sitting with his feet up on a chair, his eyes closed. I tried to slip by unnoticed.

"You okay?" his voice asked behind me. I turned. His eyes were sharp.

"People were trying to get into my room," I said.

"Tried to warn you, didn't I?"

Outside, it was still dark. Wisps of fog curled around the street lamps, and I could smell salt in the air. I shivered in the damp cold.

A young guy was fastening a poster to one of the lamp

posts. His red hair, long and tied back into a ponytail, caught the glow from the light above.

"Want to help?" he asked. "Got lots more. The faster I get them up, the sooner I can get out of here."

The poster said "Get Out of Vietnam" in red letters on a white background. Blood drops ran down from the letters.

"Sorry, no," I said. Then I stopped. The voice was vaguely familiar. I went over and looked at him more closely. "Hey, don't I know you? You're Michael Smith. You lived two doors down from us in Los Altos."

He frowned, put his finger to his lips and shook his head. He looked over his shoulder, as if checking that no one was listening.

"I'm Anne. You remember me. You were always nice to me, even though I was five and you were ten."

"You're all grown up—you're better looking than I thought you'd be. Anyway, nice meeting you, but I've got to get this done." He started to turn away.

"Michael? Do you know a place to eat around here that's open?"

He turned back. "A café over on the next street. Greasy spoon, but it's cheap."

"Thanks." I moved off into the fog. I could hear ships' horns and foghorns out in the harbour.

The café was warm and steamy, rich with the smell of coffee and toast. I ordered the breakfast special—two eggs, bacon, hash browns and toast—and was pouring three creams into my coffee when Michael walked into the café. He sat down with me.

After the waitress took his order, he said, "I'm part of the protest against Nixon's war in Vietnam."

"I wondered what happened to you. I was only in grade seven when you graduated from high school and I never saw you again."

"The last time I saw you, you had braces on your teeth. You were so skinny, your pants were falling down."

"You look about the same," I said. Freckles, front teeth with a space between them and ears that stuck out. But his chest was broader now.

"So what are you doing out on Geary Street at six in the morning on a cold, foggy day in January?" he asked. Again the nervous glance over his shoulder.

"I'm in to see the science fair. My science teacher thought I'd like to see the DNA display."

"Didn't your dad used to do research on DNA?"

"Once." I rearranged the salt and pepper shakers.

Michael drained his water glass and leaned forward. "What are you doing staying at a pimp hotel?"

"Pimp hotel? I guess that explains the secret staircase off the closet."

"No, that probably led down to a gambling room in the twenties. Most of the old hotels downtown still have them. What did you do, run away from home?"

I didn't answer.

"How did I know that? You always were a rebel. I remember the time you were about four and you took off and arrived on our doorstep with your suitcase."

"And your mother gave me milk and cookies and talked

me into going back."

His breakfast arrived, and he shook so much pepper on his eggs that I sneezed.

"Mom and Dad left for Hawaii yesterday," I said. "My grandmother was supposed to come down and stay with me a few days before they left, but there was a crisis at the school where she's headmistress. She won't be here until later today."

"So you took off for a day on your own. Sounds like something you'd do."

"I said I was going to stay the weekend with a friend from school, and I came down on the next train after classes," I said, watching him make red ketchup designs on his hash browns.

"Where's your grandmother from?"

"Victoria, BC. That's Canada."

"I know, I know. I'm heading up to Vancouver myself. That last demonstration at Berkeley? I got picked up by the cameras on the trucks outside Slater Gate."

"Are you a student at Berkeley?" I asked.

"Finished my last semester in journalism last month. I wrote for the student newspaper, and I've sold a couple of articles to the *Chronicle*."

The breakfast was delicious and the café was crowded, even at this early hour. The place buzzed with conversation and an occasional burst of laughter. Best of all, my mother was far, far away. Too far to supervise my every move.

"Hope your girlfriend covers for you if your parents happen to phone," Michael said.

"Judy? Oh, she will. But only until next week—she's moving to the Panama. Her dad's got a job there."

"You'll miss her."

"She's my best friend. I'll miss her family, too. They've taken me sailing with them ever since I've known them."

"Tough."

I leaned forward. "Michael, can I go with you to Canada?" I asked.

"Hey, whoa! How old are you, anyway? Seventeen?"

"Sixteen."

"Great. I'll get nailed for being a protestor and a draft dodger *and* for smuggling an underage female across the border. No thanks."

"I don't want to go home. Mom's always bossing me around and trying to change me. Drives me nuts."

"I remember your dad as a nice guy."

I played with the spoon on my saucer. "He feels sorry for Mom because she had a crummy childhood, so he goes along with whatever she says. Like bring Nana down here to try to get me to be the perfect little lady."

"Why not just stand up to Nana?"

"She's a headmistress, remember? She knows how to handle 'difficult young girls' like me."

Someone turned on a radio. The opening bars of the Beatles' "Hey Jude" filled the café.

Michael didn't say anything for a moment, but his eyes were sympathetic. "Well, don't let Nana break you down, Anne."

I felt a rush of gratitude. He really understood. "The next

step is to ship me up to Victoria to Nana's school. But my Aunt Ruth in Vancouver—she's my mom's sister, a black sheep, like me—she'd take me. If I can get up there."

He drew back. "Not with me. Get that out of your head."

He picked up a newspaper that someone had left on the table. "This is interesting," he said. He pointed at an article.

I glanced at the date. Friday, January 9, 1970. Yesterday. It seemed longer since I'd left home. Was my family looking for me yet?

> The World Wide liner, SS *Ocean Spirit*, due to arrive in San Francisco at Pier 35 at 2:00 p.m. tomorrow, January 10, is reported to be carrying more sick passengers and crew members. Ship authorities say it appears to be a flu-like illness.
>
> The ship has been plagued with illness since she sailed from Cherbourg on December 17. It was thought at first to be seasickness due to the rough Atlantic crossing or perhaps flu picked up in Europe during what has been described as "the worst flu epidemic in a decade."
>
> At Port Everglades in Florida, two crewmen were hospitalized. Again, at San Pedro in Los Angeles, two more crew were left behind in hospital.
>
> The ship will be departing from San Francisco at 12:00 p.m. on Monday, January 12, bound for Vancouver, Canada.

"Wonder what that's all about," I said.

"There's a story behind it, I bet you anything. If I had time, I'd check it out and write it up and sell it. If there's one thing I need, it's cash." He looked at his watch. "I have to get back, some of the other guys will be showing up by now."

"Will I see you later on, after the demonstration?"

"Anne," he said, half-laughing, "I'm twenty-two. Too old for you."

"I'll be seventeen in five months."

"That's still five years younger."

"Couldn't you be sort of my brother? You *are* in a way. You taught me to ride my two-wheeler without the training wheels."

He zipped up his jacket. "Remember how mad your mom was at both of us?" He shook his head. "No, listen, don't get any crazy ideas about me being anything more than I am. But if you're around, I'll be here for lunch around noon."

He opened the door, looked both ways, then disappeared into the fog.

The fog was still thick when I walked back to Geary Street. I thought I'd probably have time before the science fair opened to watch Michael's demonstration. But there was no demonstration—just police cars and a paddy wagon, and young men were being hustled into it, all of them protesting loudly. I stretched my neck to look for Michael.

A hand gripped my elbow. "Don't turn around. Keep your face blank." It was Michael's voice. "I need a place to lie low. Could I use your hotel room?"

I moved toward the hotel and stepped inside the doorway, and a minute later Michael joined me. He'd pulled his toque down low over his forehead, but it didn't quite cover a gash that still oozed blood.

The hotel clerk was nowhere to be seen, and Michael and I made our way up the stairs and into room 202 without meeting anyone.

"Check-out is 11:00 a.m.," I said.

"Keep it for one more night. I'll give you the cash. You're going back home this afternoon anyway, aren't you?"

I hesitated. "I guess."

"I'll need to stay here until dark." He moved to the window and closed the drapes.

"And after that?"

"Over to the marina at Sausalito. A buddy of mine is taking his cabin cruiser out on the morning tide and heading up north to Vancouver."

I felt a rush of hope. "Room for me? I wouldn't take up much."

"Not a chance in hell."

"How long are you going to be in Vancouver?"

"About a month." He took off his jacket and toque and dropped them on the carpet. "Heading over to the Kootenays after that. Let me get some sleep now. I'm going to be up all night."

"Should I come back later with some food?"

"Yeah. Chinese." He handed me a twenty. "If anybody asks you anything, just play stupid."

Downstairs I paid for one more night. A different hotel clerk was sitting there, and this one didn't even look up, just took the money with a grunt.

The police cars were still parked outside. An officer walked over to me. "What are you doing in this area?" he asked. He sounded tough.

"I'm from out of town," I said, edging away. "I'm in to see the science fair."

"You staying at that hotel?"

"Just last night."

"You know what kind of a hotel that is?"

"Noisy. And I had to push the dresser against the door." I turned to go.

"Where are you from?"

"Mountain View," I lied. Perspiration broke out on my back. What if I'd already been reported missing? "I'm going back this afternoon."

"Know any of the people demonstrating here this morning?"

"Is that what's going on? I don't know anyone around here." I tried for an innocent-looking smile. "Could you please tell me how to get to the science fair?" I showed him the brochure.

The science fair was everything I had hoped for. I started with the pictures of the landing on the moon, worked my way through an environmental display, lingered over the model of the first heart transplant and saved the DNA model for last. Dad was a microbiologist and before he went into administration with its nine-to-five schedule—which he did because Mom wanted it—his whole focus was on DNA. I loved going to the lab with him. He told me that in each cell of my body, there was a secret message, or code, written in sentences called genes, and that the code was written on a special tape called DNA. Dad was so excited to learn more about the breaking of the code that I couldn't help being excited about it too.

But I couldn't stop thinking about Michael. Even when I was studying the double helix model of DNA, the red tinker-toy components reminded me of the blood-red letters of his protest sign and the cut on his forehead. Michael had been my hero, ever since I was three and wandered down to his house one morning before anyone was up. The pepper trees hung their leaves like trailing green feathers, and the vines were full of birds going crazy with the rising sun. Michael was in his front yard, taking his bike apart. He let me stay and watch him clean and oil it.

I stayed at the science fair for hours, looking at all the exhibits. Then I took a long walk along the ocean. Already I missed Judy. She'd let me rave on about my mother until I felt better. The Panama was just too far away. What if I never saw her again?

The smells of seaweed and salt water rose from under the embankment. I watched a ship slip out from under the fog like a ghost, the Golden Gate Bridge a suspended cobweb above it. I checked my watch—twelve-thirty. That could be the ship Michael and I had read about at breakfast.

I was at Pier 35 by the time the SS *Ocean Spirit* berthed. Behind the rail barrier, I stood with the crowd and watched the gangway come out from the side and the passengers start to disembark. The ship loomed above, large as a hotel, but graceful, romantic and beautiful.

People shouted greetings, taxis honked, trucks and fork-lifts rumbled. Passengers waited at alphabetized stations to move through customs.

I was still standing behind the rail when everyone had gone. If only I could sail away on the SS *Ocean Spirit* to Vancouver! That was impossible, but at least I could hang around and maybe get some information for Michael about the flu on-board.

I was just about to leave when a small man in a business suit too tight across the shoulders came bustling over to me. "I'm the shipping agent," he said. "Are you the new utility steward?"

"No. Wish I was, though."

"Looking for work, then?"

"Yes." Yes, I was. Yes.

"You'll do. Come on. Right this way."

The next thing I knew, I was following close behind him and up a gangway. "I'm taking you to the Deucer," he said over his shoulder, and he led me to an office with "Second Steward" on a brass plaque on the door.

"This is the new US," he said to the second steward, the man sitting behind the desk. He wore a navy serge uniform with masses of silver braid round the cuff.

"Cece Rathbone," said the second steward, waving me to a chair. He took my name and began to fill out papers.

"Passport, sweetheart?"

"I haven't got it with me. I can get it, though."

"Next of kin?"

"My aunt Rosalind Miller," I said, making up a name.

"Address?"

"Thirty-two hundred Balsam Crescent, Vancouver." Another lie.

"I'll take care of the paperwork later on. Can you sign on now?"

"Yes."

"Get your passport, then, and we'll get you kitted out with a uniform from slops."

In a daze, I left the ship and started back to the hotel. I couldn't believe my luck—I had been hired and I had an escape route. Utility steward. Did that mean working in the kitchen? I hugged myself in delight. Vancouver wasn't that far away.

When I let myself into room 202, I carried a greasy paper bag full of Chinese takeout for two. But the room was empty—no note, no sign that Michael had ever been there.

I opened the closet door and then the door to the staircase. Peering down, all I could see was the narrow staircase leading into shadows. A musty odour, like mouse droppings, wafted up from the gloom.

"Michael?" I whispered.

There was a slight movement, then Michael's head and neck rose like a periscope.

"I'm alone," I said.

He came up, brushing cobwebs from his face. "A cop came about five minutes after you left. He made the hotel clerk unlock the door. Just had time to grab my stuff and hide down the staircase."

We sat side by side on the bed and shared the sweet and sour, fried rice and chow mein. As we ate, I told Michael about my job on the *Ocean Spirit.*

His chopsticks stopped midway to his mouth, and he stared at me. "You serious?"

"It's like it was meant to be. I knew I had to get away from home, that if I didn't, I'd explode."

"What're you going to do about a passport?"

"I have one, from when my family went to England last summer to visit relatives."

"And you just happen to have it with you. You've been planning this for a while."

"Always there in the back of my mind. Can we meet in Vancouver, Michael?"

"There you go again. I told you—"

"I know all about that," I said impatiently. "We're just friends, nothing more. Don't be so conceited."

He laughed.

"Thought you might like some information on the sickness on the ship, you know, for your freelance article." I tried for a matter-of-fact tone. "The ship will be in Vancouver at 7:00 a.m. on Wednesday the 14th."

Finally I had his attention. "I'll give you a phone number where I can be reached," he said. "Two-two-four, nine-eight-four-eight. Don't write it down. And if anyone asks, you don't know my last name."

"My aunt's name is Ruth Lawrence," I said. "Lives in Dunbar. She's listed in the phone book."

He leaned forward and kissed my forehead, his lips surprisingly soft. "Good luck to both of us, my friend."

All the way back to the *Ocean Spirit*, I repeated Michael's phone number until I was sure I had memorized it. The sun had finally burned away the fog, and the waters out in the bay were cobalt blue.

I stopped long enough to buy a notebook that would fit in my pocket. It would be my journal for Michael.

The closer I got to the ship, the freer I felt, and I began to run, my backpack bouncing on my shoulders. The air was cold but fresh, and I gulped it in.

I'd stay on-board until the ship left San Francisco, just in case Nana started looking for me. She must have arrived at my parents' home by now. Tomorrow was Sunday. Monday we'd sail for Vancouver and Wednesday we'd be there. I'd phone Aunt Ruth and the number Michael had given me. With any kind of luck, I'd see him then.

CHAPTER TWO

I followed Cece Rathbone along the highly polished lino of the passageway, so shiny that it looked like water.

"Your cabin's in the passenger section. Closer to the hospital," he said. "In an emergency, you're handy."

"I thought I was working in the kitchen."

"The nurses need help," he said. "What with this flu all over the ship. Any experience?"

"I worked as a candy striper at the local hospital."

"Sounds good. Candy stripper."

"Striper," I said.

"Right you are." His smile was sly.

He knocked at C115. When there was no answer, he unlocked the door with one of many keys on a huge ring clipped to his belt.

The cabin was small and compact and had a porthole with a white cone allowing fresh air to come in. I looked around: a wardrobe, a sink, a dressing table and an upper and lower bunk. The scent of perfume lingered in the cabin.

"You're sharing with Tracey Hunt. She works in the child

centre. We've pulled her to work in the hospital, too. You both start tomorrow morning." He measured me with his eyes. "You wear an eight, sweetheart?"

"Ten."

"Main hospital's midship, C Deck. Crew's mess on D, one deck down, Annie."

"Anne."

"That's what I said, isn't it?"

I had trouble finding the crew's mess, and no one was around to ask. They must have all gone ashore.

The mess was a bare room with water pipes running overhead. Four men sat on black plastic chairs at a long table. All of the furniture was fastened to the deck with short chains.

Four pairs of eyes swung my way as I walked to the food, which was kept warm in a heated serving unit. Roast pork and gravy, mixed veg, mashed potatoes. But no cutlery.

One of the men got up from the table and came over. "Hi," he said. "Can I help?" He was about twenty, with thick dark hair and a bony face in need of a shave.

"I can't find the knives and forks."

He opened a cupboard and brought out a stainless steel knife, fork and tablespoon wrapped in a paper napkin. "These are yours now. You need to take them with you when you go." He set them on my tray. "When you're finished, you wash them in one of the pails in the sinks." He gestured toward a row of sinks near the door. Then he filled a glass from the ice-water tap and placed it beside my cutlery.

"Thank you," I said and went to an empty table near the

sinks at the back. A rim of hinged wood ran all around the table, the same as on Judy's sailboat—a fiddle, her dad called it.

Two men sauntered into the mess carrying their cutlery. "Hear that Mac and Harvey were taken ashore a couple of hours ago," said one to the other.

"That so? Thought they were sick."

"Sick enough to be in a 'Frisco hospital." They joined the men at the other table.

I ate quickly and took my cutlery over to the sinks. A pail of scummy water sat in one sink, and two dirty towels hung on nails above. My mother would have a fit. "No wonder there's flu on-board," she would say. I rinsed my cutlery under running water, dried each piece with the corner of my shirt and rewrapped them in the napkin.

My roommate, Tracey Hunt, was in the cabin when I got back, and now the scent of perfume was stronger. About eighteen with a quick, bright smile and a dimple on the top of each cheek, she looked calm and unflappable. She was from Sydney, Australia, she said. "Great life, this, other than missing Mum and Dad at Christmas. First time I've been away at Christmas time. Wonder how we'll get along with Sister B. tomorrow."

"B?"

"As in …" She grinned. "She trained in one of the big London hospitals. Friend of mine, one of the cleaning staff, says Sister makes him vacuum the keyholes. Mind if I have the lower berth?"

"No, fine with me."

Tracey handed me a package done up in white paper. "Cece Rathbone left a couple of uniforms for you. How come you rate special service? Everybody else has to pick up their working clothes at the slop chest, and they dock your first paycheque."

I hung the uniforms in the wardrobe and began to put away my few things in a drawer.

"You want to come to the Harlem Globetrotters with us tonight?" Tracey asked. "One of the passengers gave me tickets. I've got one extra if you like."

"I should get to bed early, I didn't get much sleep last night." Safer to stay on-board in case Nana was already looking for me.

"You can always sleep," she scoffed. "Our motto is, Work hard and play hard."

"Did you say the Harlem Globetrotters?"

She waved the ticket in front of my face.

"I'd *love* to go."

Tracey sat down and began to repair a broken nail. "You want to borrow any clothes? Notice you didn't bring much stuff."

"I left home in kind of a hurry."

She looked up. "Trouble at home?"

"Sort of." I didn't meet her eyes.

"Oh, you poor thing," she said cheerfully.

"I'll just wear my jeans," I hurried to say. "But thanks."

Six of us took a cab to the game. "Meet my new mate," Tracey said, introducing me to three male crew—one of them her boyfriend—and Emily, who worked in the hair salon. Emily had long, chestnut hair that she tossed every few minutes.

"Hey, hold that," said Tracey. "You got me in the eye that time."

"Sorry," said Emily, tossing her hair again.

"Anne and I have already met," said one of the men. "In the crew's mess."

I looked at him. "Sorry—I didn't recognize you."

"Bob Miller. I work in the engine room. Stoker."

It was the man who had supplied me with the cutlery. He had shaved and shampooed and was good-looking. Not that I was interested. Four more days and I'd be in Vancouver, getting in touch with Aunt Ruth and Michael. I wondered if Michael had made it safely across to Sausalito and the cabin cruiser.

At the game I sat between Joe, Tracey's boyfriend, and Bob. The game was incredible. One of the players, over seven feet tall and with legs like stilts, sank three baskets in the first fifteen minutes.

At halftime we all stood up to stretch and get something to eat. That's when I saw her—a girl I'd gone to school with—three rows ahead of us. I grabbed Bob's arm and pulled him back to sit beside me.

"What's the matter?" he asked. "You look spooked."

"Stay with me," I whispered. "I'll explain later."

I waited until the girl had gone up the aisle. "It's someone from home," I said.

"And?"

"I don't want to be seen."

He gave me a funny look, and then he said, "What you need is a disguise."

"Like what?"

He searched the pockets of his jean jacket and came up with a large red bandana and a pair of safety glasses from the engine room. Dried perspiration showed white in the red fabric and felt sticky in my hand. I tied it on, pirate fashion.

"Pull it lower down on your forehead," Bob said. "Okay, now the glasses. Yeah, that should do it. Ready to go?"

"I don't look like me?"

"Nope. Not nearly as pretty."

The girl was nowhere to be seen, and some of the tension went out of my shoulders. If an old schoolmate recognized me here in San Francisco, it would be such a coincidence that she'd talk about it to everyone, and it would get back to Nana. I decided to stay on-board the *Ocean Spirit* until we sailed. I couldn't afford to take any more chances.

When we got back to the ship, Tracey said to me in a low voice, "Do you mind letting me have the cabin for about an hour?"

"I have a choice?"

"Thanks, Anne. I'll do the same for you someday."

Bob waited for me. "Want to go for a mug-up?"

"Sounds good." I had an hour to kill.

We sat in the galley between the first class and tourist dining rooms, and a steward bounded through the swinging doors with trays of desserts left over from the passengers' buffet: pies, cakes, trifles, tortes, fruit, cheeses, crackers.

"I could get used to this," I said.

"Hey, Robert," called an older man from the end of the table. "How come you get to sit with the new lassie?"

"Guess I live right, Sandy."

"Any more scuttlebutt about the typhoid scare?" Sandy asked the steward.

"That was a bombshell, all right."

Typhoid? "What? What?" I asked.

The steward set down another plate of pastries. "When we sailed from Los Angeles, a launch came out after us and a company agent said we had typhoid aboard. Captain announced it at dinner, told the passengers they would be vaccinated in 'Frisco, and talk about panic! Mrs. Guiness, she's in first class and a royal pain in the butt, had hysterics."

Bob turned to me. "Both of the crew we left behind in LA were cabinmates of mine. Don't look so shocked. The captain found out this morning that the diagnosis was a mistake. It's not typhoid."

"So what is it?"

"Salmonella or dysentery, they say."

Sunday to Wednesday—no, I'd have to count today. That made five days. Sailing on the SS *Ocean Spirit* to Vancouver no longer seemed like such a good idea.

CHAPTER THREE

The midships hospital, a clinic in the centre of the ship where Cece Rathbone sent me, was not what I had expected. It was small and white, with two two-bed wards, a four-bed ward and a three-bed ward. Almost all of the beds were occupied by patients suffering from what looked like a bad case of flu. Each bed was bolted to the deck and had sides that could be put up during heavy seas. Most of the patients in the midships hospital were men, many of them dark-skinned.

A tall, angular woman with a flowing white square folded into a band across her forehead and pinned tightly behind her neck came toward Tracey and me. "I am the sister-in-charge," she said to me. "What is your name?"

"Anne McLaughlin-Scott."

"Anne McLaughlin-Scott, Sister." She waited.

"Anne McLaughlin-Scott, Sister."

"The top button on your uniform is undone."

My fingers fumbled to close it. Cece Rathbone had given me a size eight and I'd realized it too late.

"You are really very young," she continued, her eyes boring into mine. "You came aboard in San Francisco?"

"Yes, Sister."

"Unusual."

I kept my eyes on hers. "No, Sister."

She sniffed in disdain. "Be that as it may. Follow me."

She led us to a small utility room off to one side. "You must wash your hands between patients and after handling any contaminated material. Now, pay strict attention."

She turned on the faucet by pushing the lever with her elbow and used a foot pedal to pump green soap from a dispenser into her hands. When she had lathered her hands, she took a small brush and scrubbed them, paying particular attention to her nails and scrubbing right up to her elbows. She rinsed and dried her hands on a paper towel.

"Show me," she commanded.

I went first, wondering why we didn't just wear disposable gloves, the way Dad did at his lab. My hands were pink and stinging by the time Sister was satisfied.

"Your button's undone again. That uniform is at least a size too small."

She pulled a folded patient gown from a linen shelf and ordered me to cover myself with it. I put it on.

Back in the utility room, Sister pointed out a shiny steel apparatus. "The bedpans are rinsed and sterilized in this hopper," she said. "And you will never, ever, carry a bedpan without its cover. Any questions?"

"No, Sister," Tracey and I said together.

"Next, patient care. Follow me," she said, striding away.

"We'll start with Mr. Ayub Naidoo. He's a forty-two-year-old man from Goa, India, who works as a stoker in the boiler room. He came down with flu-like symptoms last night, temperature of 101 and a rash on his upper trunk. He has a history of a few days of constipation, then diarrhea."

We stepped into the three-bed ward and Sister smiled, all teeth displayed. "Mr. Naidoo," she said loudly, "I want to show these two young aides how to give patient care."

She started to pull down the sheet. The man clutched at it, eyes wide.

Without lowering her voice, Sister B. said, "I don't think he understands English." She motioned to Mr. Naidoo to turn on his side and when he didn't, she yanked the sheet from his hands and rolled him over like a log. He farted. The smell was foul.

"Miss McLaughlin-Scott," Sister said, "you'll find a basin, alcohol and talc in the bottom of the bedside locker. Fill the basin with warm water. Miss Hunt, fetch a draw sheet and a couple of blue pads from the linen shelves."

After Sister showed us how to wash Mr. Naidoo's back and rub it with alcohol, she loosened the soiled draw sheet—a narrower sheet of heavier cotton—and rolled it toward the middle, under his hips. Tucking one end of the clean sheet under the mattress, she smoothed the draw sheet toward the middle of the bed and made a tight roll.

"Go to the other side of the bed, Miss McLaughlin-Scott," she ordered. It was easy to roll Mr. Naidoo in the opposite direction, pull out the dirty draw sheet, then pull through the clean one.

"Patient care also includes making sure the patient has fresh water. Empty the urinal, measure and record the amount and colour on the list in the utility room."

"Colour, Sister?" I said.

"Straw, amber, dark, orange. Cloudy, clear. All of it is important information."

We washed our hands and moved on to the next patient.

"Mr. Dombrosky is an engineer," Sister said, her hand at his wrist, her eyes on her watch. "His temperature was 100 early this morning, and he was put on an antibiotic. As you can see, he has profuse diaphoresis. He will need to be sponged and the bed changed. Miss McLaughlin-Scott, let me see you do that."

Profuse diaphoresis turned out to mean sweating heavily. Everything was damp—his gown, his skin, the sheets. And so was I, by the time I had finished.

Sister followed me into the utility room and watched me empty Mr. Dombrosky's urinal into a measuring cup and hold it up to the light. Definitely not straw-coloured. "Amber?" I said, tentatively.

"Yes, it's concentrated because he's been perspiring. Empty the container down the bedpan hopper and rinse the urinal. Wash your hands."

Mr. Haywood was next. "He's a passenger, Australian, on his way home to Sydney," Sister said. Another nurse appeared at the doorway and beckoned. Thrusting the patient's chart into my hand, Sister hurried to join her and the two disappeared.

I opened the chart and began to read the history sheet.

> This 63-year-old gentleman developed a febrile illness beginning on January 1st, 1970, characterized by malaise, high temperatures, anorexia, and sweating. He was thought to have influenza and was given a short course of oral Penicillin, which did not improve him. Two weeks after onset, he still had his fever, anorexia, and some abdominal cramps and mild diarrhea. He was placed on Tetracycline 1 gram daily for five days, and he appears to be improving.

"What *are* you doing?" Sister barked from right beside me. I jumped. "The contents of that chart are none of your business." She snatched it from my hand. "Take the green soap and bleach containers from the utility room to the dispensary and have them refilled. Be quick about it."

I looked to Tracey for guidance. "Aft hospital," she mouthed, pointing toward the back of the ship.

Every bed in that hospital was occupied, too. Somehow I found the dispensary and the dispenser—a young man with strong features who wore black pants, a white shirt open at the neck and a black tie that dangled to one side. He was pinning negatives on a line over a sink, amid a strong smell of developing fluid.

"Hello, luv," he said. "I'll be with you in a minute."

It gave me a chance to look around. A black jacket with brass buttons hung on a hook on the back of the door. On the shoulder was an insignia, gold on a red background. Racks over a glass-topped bench held small bottles that sat in holes in the shelves. Below the dispensing bench were cupboards, and next to them, a sterilizer hissed.

"They call me the dizzy," he said, "short for dispenser. But my real name is Henry Dixon. You must be the new lass."

I nodded. "Sister sent me for bleach and green soap for the midships hospital. She told me to be quick about it."

"Oh, you must mean Frosty Face." He took the containers to the large store cupboard nearby to refill them. "How do you like working in a hospital aboard ship? I'd say by the looks of you that you should be behind a desk in high school. Junior grade, at that." His eyes behind the glasses were sharp. He seemed already to know everything about me that was worth knowing.

I began to stammer an answer.

"Don't let my joshing get to you. You'll do fine. Any way I can help, you let me know."

"Do you have a book where I could look up things, like salmonella and dysentery?"

"Is that the latest diagnosis?" He gave me two books, a faded brown *Microbiology and Pathology* and a well-thumbed *Ship Captain's Medical Guide*. "Only one rule. You have to look at them here."

I looked up salmonella and dysentery, read the short sections and made notes. The two diseases seemed related. "I wonder how this sickness is spreading," I said.

"I heard tell 'tis in the water," he said, tapping the side of his nose with his forefinger.

"Who told you?"

"Them as knows."

I waited, hoping he'd say more, but he turned away. "I'd best finish making up those eye drops," he said. He picked up a tiny bottle filled with a strange mixture of yellow and green powder and weighed out a small amount. With a spatula he pulled from his shirt pocket, he added a little more powder on the scale until he was satisfied. "Three hundred milligrams of fluorescein sodium dissolved in 15 millilitres of water gives a two-percent aqueous solution," he explained.

"*Green* eye drops?"

"For diagnostics. Shows up on t'cornea if there's damage," he said.

"Oh. Yes."

"What a day!" said Tracey as we walked back to our cabin after supper. "My feet are killing me."

"I wonder what's causing the sickness."

"Scuttlebutt has it that it's in the food," Tracey said.

Suddenly the supper I'd eaten seemed heavy in my stomach.

"Are you sure you won't come to Chinatown with us?" Tracey asked. "Take your mind off sickness and Sister."

"I've got a couple of letters to write. Besides, I'm beat."

"Bob will be there," Tracey said. She outlined her lips with a lip pencil and brushed on a poppy-pink shade.

"I already have a boyfriend." I wish.

"Different rules at sea." She ran the tip of her little finger along her lips, blending in the lipstick.

"No, thanks," I said.

As soon as she left, I began to wish I'd gone—the cabin was too small and lonely. I decided to explore the ship and make a few notes, perhaps even sketch out the layout of the ship for Michael.

I started with a diagram of the ship, posted near the first-class dining room. It showed the location of each deck, the bridge with its wheelhouse, and even named the different masts. Right next to the diagram was a rack of brochures describing the *Ocean Spirit*. I chose a few of them for my journal. I even found back copies of the ship's daily newsletter and tucked them away in my pockets for Michael.

The plan of the *Ocean Spirit* showed nine passenger decks. At the top was the Sun Deck, below that was A Deck, or Boat Deck, then B Deck, C Deck, and so on down to H Deck, which was below the waterline and had no portholes. Galleys and pantries were situated near the first-class dining room. I wondered if I could somehow get in to see them. What if I could discover something? I had a small camera in my backpack, and I went back to my cabin to get it.

And found Cece Rathbone knocking at my door. "Oh, there you are, sweetheart. Settling in all right, are you? Anything I can do for you?"

"No. No thanks." I opened the door just enough to slip in, closed it with a quick click behind me and locked it. I could hear Cece breathing on the other side. It seemed forever before his footsteps faded away.

When I was sure he'd gone, I left my cabin and went to the crew's mess. There the pantry steward I'd met the evening before was cleaning the tables, and I asked him if I could see the galley and pantries.

"I guess so," he said, "but it's wipe-it-down time."

"I'll keep out of the way," I promised.

He showed me the pantries, near the galley. "We pass

the food to the wingers who serve it to the bloods," said the steward.

"Sounds like a good job to me," I said, thinking of Sister and bedpans.

"The best jobs are the salad room, the still room and the cold meats room. The worst is the toast machine." He pointed to the toast machine which was about four feet long and two and a half feet high—the size of a fridge turned on its side—and set on a waist-high table. "You put the bread on the hooks on the belt and take it off when it comes through."

"Why is that so bad?"

"In the tropics, the heat is bloody awful. We sweat like pigs. That's why we take salt tablets. The dizzy says there's glucose in them, too, for nausea. We take three or four a day."

I took a picture of the large stone jar of tablets, making sure that my camera was focused on the large water tank beside it. Tracey had said it was the food, but Henry Dixon seemed to think it was the water.

"Who drinks from that water tank besides the pantry stewards?" I asked, rolling the film forward.

"The passengers. The wingers fill the thermos jugs for the dining room from it," he said. "Why?"

"I heard something about the water being the reason that everyone was getting sick."

"I think it's the ice cream. I won't touch it myself. It's either that or the hamburgers. They're what the crew usually eat."

I stayed to chat with the pantry steward, asking about the trip, the crew and anything else that might help Michael with his article about the sickness on-board.

2030 hrs. Sat. Jan. 10 On-board the SS Ocean Spirit. British-owned, 21 knot, 28,000 ton, 19 years old, white hull, 1 yellow funnel with black "Welch Cap" cap on top.

Sailed from Southampton on Dec. 17 for Cherbourg, Madeira, Spain, Bermuda, Port Everglades, Nassau, Cristobal, Balboa, Acapulco, Los Angeles, San Francisco.

Stowaway put off at Madeira.

2 crew men hospitalized at Port Everglades, Florida, 2 men in Los Angeles, 4 in San Francisco. Total of 12 patients in both ship's hospitals.

Symptoms: constipation or diarrhea, fever, headache, muscle pain.

Diagnosis: flu, gastroenteritis.

Treatment: Clear fluids, IV's.

Medication: Antibiotics.

Occupation: Engineers, mostly, some pantrymen.

Nationality: European, Goanese.

CHAPTER FOUR

Monday. Departure day. A rosy sunrise, and a brisk breeze that tugged at the mooring lines and made the mast, with its radar scanner, sing. With the taste of salt in the air, I felt like singing, too.

Even Sister B. was affected, and the slight twitch at her lips when I reported for duty could have been a smile.

"I see you've got on a uniform that fits decently. As soon as you've cleared away the breakfast trays, start your patient care with Mr. Naidoo; he's the sickest."

Tracey had been sent to work in the aft hospital. "Wish me luck," she'd said at breakfast. "At least I don't have Sister B."

Sister came in to see how I was doing with Mr. Naidoo. She frowned when she saw how I'd made his bed. "Hospital corners, Miss McLaughlin-Scott," she said, ripping out the sheets. "Pay close attention." She showed me how to pull the bottom sheet taut, tuck it in, mitre the corner and fold it under the mattress so that it looked like an envelope. She made me do it over and over until she was satisfied.

Eleven patients to be bathed. I smoothed fluffs of baby

powder over freshly washed backs, offered water for shaving, peppermint mouthwash, toothbrushes, combs. I refilled the thermoses at the patients' bedsides with ice water. Emptied, measured and recorded the contents of urinals.

"You can take your coffee break now," said Sister in mid-morning. I had almost reached the door, already anticipating the rich taste of the ship's coffee, when two doctors came in.

"Stay," Sister said to me. "I want to make rounds with the surgeons."

"You have an aide, I see," said the older doctor to Sister, sounding pleased. He had cut himself shaving and patched it with a small piece of tissue. "You need the help."

"That's the theory. Not that she's that much help, Dr. Smythe. I spend more time trying to train her than it would take to do it myself."

"Now, now, Sister," said the younger doctor. He was dark-haired, serious and good-looking, and the lime scent of his aftershave made my mouth water. "Another pretty face in here will do the patients a world of good." He winked at me. "Let's have a look at Mr. Ayub Naidoo."

"Yes, Dr. Connor."

"And let the aide accompany us. The more she knows, the more helpful she'll be." He smiled at Sister. Sister did not smile back.

On my coffee break, I went up to the top deck. On the pier below was a blackboard.

THE SS OCEAN SPIRIT

WILL SAIL AT 12 O'CLOCK FOR VANCOUVER

I scanned the pier, half-afraid of seeing Nana. It would be just like her to have phoned the family I said I was staying with. I shivered. Two more hours to go.

I left the bright sunlight and fresh sea air tinged with the smells of roasting coffee, iodine, rope, diesel fuel and tar, and went inside to artificial lighting and air conditioning that circulated stale cigarette smoke and whiffs of expensive perfume. Past passengers leaving the dining room with satiated looks on their faces. Into the hospital with its white surfaces and the smell of disinfectant not quite masking the odour of feces.

An imposing-looking officer with wide gold epaulettes had just walked up to Sister. He was solid, with hands big as boxing gloves, a tanned face and piercing blue eyes. He had to be the captain.

"I need a word with you, Sister," he said. "In private, please."

"Yes, Captain Bunyon. In the treatment room."

I went to the linen shelves, near enough to hear but not be seen, and began to tidy the stacks of gowns, towels and smooth, ironed sheets.

"I've radioed San Pedro and San Francisco," the captain said, "and asked them to confirm the diagnosis on the crew we landed there. I hear one thing, but I suspect another."

"Yes, sir."

"I've decided to take no chances," he said. "Passengers and crew are to receive anti-typhoid vaccinations immediately, starting with the crew."

"Yes, sir."

"A Mr. and Mrs. Guiness from first class will be coming to you shortly for their inoculations. I want you to reassure them that we are doing everything possible."

"Yes, sir."

A patient called out, "Nurse!" and I hurried to his room. I was just leaving the ward with his bedpan when Sister and the captain walked out of the treatment room. The captain glanced around, taking everything in, including me.

Sister went to a cupboard and took out a box of small vials, placed it on a tray, added alcohol wipes and a box of sterile syringes with needles. "Miss Scott," she called loudly as she worked. I guessed that was me, minus half my name.

"Yes, Sister," I said, behind her.

"Good heavens! Why are you sneaking up like that?"

"I'm sorry, Sister."

She added a small basin to the tray and pulled the wastebasket closer. "After I give each shot, I want you to check off the name. Ask Mr. Rathbone to supply us with the names of all the passengers."

"And crew?"

"No," she said. "They will be vaccinated in the crew surgery by Mr. Dixon and the assistant surgeon. The riffraff do not hobnob with the passengers."

I found a list of phone numbers beside the wall phone. Cece Rathbone answered after the first ring. "Oh, it's you, sweetheart. Wondered when you'd phone."

My hand tightened on the receiver. I gave him Sister's message, trying not to sound as irritated as I felt.

Just then, the Guinesses came in. She was fluttery, he

indignant. "What is the meaning of all this? We paid for a first-class ticket on a first-class line and now, trouble."

"The typhoid report was false," Sister soothed. "And we have the flu situation well in hand."

"Flu be damned," said Mr. Guiness. "Even a fool would know this is more than flu."

"Mrs. Guiness," said Sister. "If you will sit here and roll up your sleeve, we'll give you your typhoid vaccination. It's purely precautionary, of course." I watched her unwrap a sterile syringe, attach a needle, break open the vial and draw up the small amount of vaccine. She wiped Mrs. Guiness's arm with an alcohol swab before giving her the shot.

When it came to his turn, Mr. Guiness paled. He extended his arm to Sister and closed his eyes, and his lips moved as if in prayer.

"Fetch Mr. Guiness a drink of water, Miss Scott," said Sister.

The first chance I got, I went to the crew surgery, hoping to find something that Michael could use in his article. A long line of crew members waited outside of the surgery: cooks, pantrymen, bellboys and crew from the engine room. Bob was among them. "You should have been here a minute ago," he said. "You know Tanky, the winchman? He's one tough customer. Fainted out here while waiting."

"Where's he now?"

"Inside."

As he spoke, Tanky appeared from behind the door and rejoined his mates. They gave him a rousing cheer.

"He'll never live that down," said Bob. "Looks like I'm next."

I sniffed at an aroma of spices in the air. "Something smells good," I said.

"It's goat curry from the Indian crew's galley under the fo'c'sle head. They have their own galley, and so do the European crew. Some trips we carry a live sheep to be slaughtered for curry for their Ramadan festival."

"Wish I could have some right now."

"There's a good movie tonight in the crew's rec room," Bob said. "*Sound of Music*. See you there?"

Later that morning, Sister sent me to the dispensary. "Ask Mr. Dixon for another box of one-inch, 22-gauge needles." While I was there, an announcement blared over the loudspeakers. "Would visitors please repair ashore as the ship is about to sail."

"Why not nip up on deck and watch the ship leave?" Henry Dixon said. "It's something you don't want to miss."

I ran up the short flight of stairs that led from the dispensary to the upper deck. The Blue Peter flag, a white square on a blue background, snapped from the foremast. Tracey had told me at breakfast that the flag was raised when the ship was under sailing orders.

The wharf workers shouted good-natured insults to the ship's crew as they stood ready to let loose the mooring lines. The deckhands gave as good as they got. Friends and relatives of the passengers stood on the pier and waved goodbye. Streamers were thrown toward the pier in response, until the ship looked like a New Year's party. A small band thumped away.

I watched fresh fruits and vegetables being chain-ganged by the ship's utility stewards up the gangways, the produce disappearing into the ship. Fresh-water hoses and shore phone lines were disconnected. A command came over a loudspeaker: "Single up forward and aft," followed by, "let go springs." And then, "Cast off forward, cast off aft." The wharfies dropped the lines, *splerdoosh*, and we were on our way.

The ship's whistle sounded three times. The turbine engines throbbed beneath me, a steady thrum that caused the deck to vibrate gently. Slowly the ship reversed, a tug on either side to help nudge her away from the pilings. The space between the ship and the wharf widened. I turned to look out to the Golden Gate Bridge and the open sea that lay beyond. Once we were out there, I would breathe easier.

But I didn't dare linger on deck. Sister was probably counting the minutes I was away. I ran back down to the dispensary, where Henry Dixon had the needles waiting for me. "I figured you'd want to look up typhoid now," he said, handing me a book that he had opened to the right spot.

"I'd like to make a few notes," I said, reaching for a piece of scrap paper. He had been sorting through a stack of enlargements, and now he handed me a photo of a pretty, dark-haired girl sitting on a beach near a sailing dinghy. "Here's the girl I'm going to marry," he said. "She lives in Tassie."

"Tassie?"

"Tasmania, an island state of Australia, 130 miles south of Victoria. Lots of sunny beaches and not many people. We're getting married soon—this is my last trip."

"Won't you miss the shipboard life?"

"Yes, but if I stay, I run the risk of becoming either an alcoholic or a sex maniac."

"Oh … Well, I'd better go. Sister will kill me."

"Taaraa, luv."

By the end of the shift, Sister reported to Dr. Connor that most of the crew and a few of the passengers had been inoculated against typhoid. "Has the aide had her shot?" he asked.

"We've been so busy I forgot to ask her," she said, putting away the unused vials of vaccine. She handed me the wastebasket full of empty vials, used syringes, needles and alcohol swabs. "Empty this," she said.

I stood still, thinking. I wasn't sure if I had been vaccinated against typhoid. My mother was always cautious about everything, and I knew she didn't trust inoculations, ever since an uncle of hers had almost died after having one for smallpox.

Dr. Connor's voice brought me back. "Well, let's ask her now. Miss …"

"McLaughlin-Scott," I supplied.

"Have you been vaccinated against typhoid?" His tie was blue with tiny red dots, like pinpricks.

"I don't know. But wouldn't it take a while after a shot for an immunity to build up?"

He nodded, his eyes sharpening. "About a month after the first of a series of shots."

"So, isn't it all kind of futile?"

Sister made a choking sound. "Miss McLaughlin-Scott, empty that wastebasket. Now."

I turned, a sour taste of humiliation in my mouth.

Behind me, the doctor said, "She's right, you know, Sister. It is futile."

The movie had already started, but Bob had saved a seat for me. I hadn't been sitting beside him long before I realized that his body was burning with fever. I peered through the darkness at him, then touched his forehead.

"You've got a temperature," I said.

"Probably from the shot."

"How do you feel?"

"Headache. Tight chest."

"Let's go," I said, standing up and taking his hand. "You should see the doctor."

"I'm okay."

"You either come with me, or I'll yell rape."

"Jesus, Anne!"

But he got up, and when we were standing outside the theatre in brighter light, I was glad I'd insisted. He was trembling, and his face was white with a sheen of perspiration.

Dr. Connor took him into the treatment room. While I stood waiting, another crew member came into the hospital. "I ache all over," he told the evening nurse. "Must be coming down with the granddaddy of all bugs."

The nurse turned to me. "Could you be a lamb and put together a chart for him? You'll find the paperwork in the bottom drawer there. This place is a zoo tonight!"

Dr. Connor admitted Bob to one of the hospital beds. When I went in to see Bob, he said, "New patient who just came in? From my cabin. That makes four of us now, out of ten. Six to go."

Tracey was in our cabin when I got back, and I told her about Bob. Her eyes widened. After a few moments, she said, "I almost forgot—Cece Rathbone wants to see you."

"Too bad." I began to brush my hair.

"He says it's important."

"How important?"

"Sister B. has been to see him about you. If I were you, I'd trot along. You can't just get off the ship and catch a bus out of here, you know."

I went up to B Deck, meeting passengers on their way to the fancy costume ball: clowns, princesses, even a cow with brown and white patches.

Cece was in his office, and when I knocked, he looked up from his desk, leaned back and lit up a strong-smelling cigarette. "Like one?" he offered.

"I'm too young to smoke."

"Well, sweetie, you've got yourself into a bit of trouble. Not that I don't like a bit of spunk in a woman."

I didn't answer, but waited.

He raised his eyebrows. "Sister has been in to see me, wanted to see your personnel record. Thinks you're a runaway and that your family should be notified.

I stared him down. I'd put down my aunt as my nearest relative and had given a phony name and address.

Cece examined the tip of his cigarette. "I told Sister that all of your papers were in the office in San Francisco. Didn't mention the copy I have here." He tapped the front of a filing cabinet, paused and looked at me. "One small favour deserves another in return. What say you?"

"That sixteen is too young to be asked for favours. There's a law against it." If there wasn't, there should be.

He stubbed out his cigarette and waved his hand in dismissal. "Don't say I didn't warn you."

I left, shaking with anger.

When I told Tracey about it, she said, "Don't get your knickers in a knot. Cece tries it with all the new girls."

"He's such an ugly little man—who would possibly want him?" I said in disgust. "I'm going up on deck to get some fresh air."

It was cold on deck and the night was bright with starlight. I found a sheltered spot out of the wind and looked up at the sky, marvelling at how thick the stars were away from the lights of the city. The ship felt alive beneath me and I felt some magical part of it.

For the first time since leaving home, I relaxed. Whatever happened, I would soon be in Vancouver—away from home, away from my mother and her poking and prodding, always wanting to know what I thought and then telling me why I shouldn't think it.

I looked out to where the sea ended and the sky began. The waves were long and rolling. Was Michael out there somewhere, going up one side of a wave and down the other?

"Chilly evening to be out, Miss," said a man's voice beside me. A ship's officer with a long face, gentle and melancholy as a hound's, stood beside me. "I'm third mate, Dennis Wilson."

"And I'm Anne," I said. He thought I was a passenger.

We talked. No, he talked. About his mother and sister back in Hull. About their Irish retriever, Ben. About going to church every Sunday, mid-week, too. As he talked about home, his face became like a young boy's.

Finally I told him that I worked in the hospital as an aide. And without meaning to, but tired of keeping it all bottled in, I told him about my family and said that I'd run away. "But you have to promise not to tell anyone," I said, "because I'm leaving the ship in Vancouver. Don't look so concerned! I have an aunt who lives there."

"You're so young. Your family must be worried."

"I guess."

"You should phone them as soon as you're settled. Promise you'll do that."

This was not what I wanted to hear. "Would you mind walking me to my cabin, Dennis? There's this—uh, guy—who's been bothering me."

"Of course." He took my arm to guide me toward the stairs.

At the door, Dennis ducked his head, as if he were going to kiss me. But it was an awkward bow, the last thing in the world I expected. No one had ever bowed to me before.

"I'll see you again, I hope," he said.

2200 hrs. Mon. Jan. 12, 1970. On-board SS Ocean Spirit. Sailed from San Francisco at 1200 hrs. with 900 passengers and 600 crew on-board.

12 pts. in hospital when we sailed, 2 new admissions by 2100 hrs. Both Caucasian, both work in the engine room, shared same cabin. Tetracycline 1 gram daily x 5 ordered. (Oral Penicillin used with earlier admissions.)

Typhoid bacilli: gram-negative, contacted by swallowing food or water contaminated by feces or urine of infected carrier or person ill of the disease, incubation period 7-14 days.

CHAPTER FIVE

"Tell me, Miss McLaughlin-Scott," Sister said the next morning as soon as I walked through the door. "Where did you say your parents live?"

"I didn't say, Sister."

Her eyebrows rose.

"They're both dead." God forgive me for even saying it.

"Oh."

"In a car accident, two years ago."

"I'm sorry to hear that. Have you been living with relatives?"

"No, a friend of the family's. She teaches at Stanford." My face was getting hot.

Dr. Connor joined us.

"What does this friend teach?" Sister persisted.

Could she smell my fear? Even the backs of my knees were wet with perspiration. "English literature. Modern poetry."

"Like Wordsworth."

Was she trying to trick me? Even I knew that Wordsworth was a Romantic. "No, her dissertation was on Wallace Stevens, an American."

"I've never heard of him." Her eyes fixed me as if I were an insect to be examined.

"Sister," said Dr. Connor quietly. "What is the new admission's temperature?"

"Robert Miller? It came down during the night, but it's started to climb again."

"The Tetracycline should kick in soon."

I went to see Bob. He wasn't as pale as he'd been the evening before. "I think I feel a bit better," he said.

As I washed his back with a warm, soapy face cloth, I was surprised at how long it was, and—in spite of the muscles—how vulnerable it looked. I liked taking care of sick people. I could be a nurse. Science *and* people. But I'd have to finish high school first. I couldn't wait to phone Aunt Ruth, go and live with her, and get back to school.

I went to the fridge to get a can of ginger ale for Bob. If typhoid was carried through contaminated food and water, canned pop would be safer. I'd decided at breakfast that I wouldn't even drink the ship's milk any more. Tracey had told me that some of it was reconstituted, so instead of my usual cereal, I'd had sausages, toast and tea.

About an hour later, the captain and the senior surgeon Dr. Smythe came in, their faces serious. "Sister, Dr. Connor," said Captain Bunyon. "San Francisco has just radiophoned, 'Typhoid confirmed.' I have informed the passengers, and those who did not receive vaccine yesterday are to receive it today."

Shortly after he left, passengers began to arrive, and they were visibly upset. The men demanded vaccinations right away. One young woman sobbed desperately. When I went to her, she grabbed my arm, her fingernails sharp in my skin. "Oh, let me be first! I have children."

I comforted her as best I could, then went back to Sister and Dr. Smythe.

"Carry on, Sister, with your regular duties," Dr. Smythe said. "Dr. Connor and I will take over the vaccinations."

Sister set up the tray for the surgeons: vaccine, needles and alcohol swabs. I fetched the wastebasket and the passenger list.

A typhoid epidemic. I couldn't help but think of the Dark Ages and the plagues that we'd studied at school. Twenty-four more hours to go before we'd be in Vancouver. I planned to be off the ship and running as soon as she docked.

All day long, passengers came into the hospital. "I'm sure I already have typhoid," said one middle-aged woman. "I have these palpitations. They start here—" she indicated her heart region—"and they go all the way down and across here," and she pointed to her abdomen.

"Appetite all right?" asked Dr. Connor.

"Oh, yes." Her pupils were dilated with fear.

"Any changes in your bowel habits? Constipated? Diarrhea?"

"No, nothing like that."

He gave her a shot of the vaccine and two pills in a small vial. "This is a mild tranquillizer," he said. "Take one the next time you have palpitations and, if necessary, another one eight hours later. If you don't get any relief, come back and see me."

In the crew's mess, we had a choice of filet mignon, quail,

salmon fillet or pork tenderloin in cream—all entrees from the first-class dining room. "Passengers are afraid to eat," the steward told me.

So was I. I chose prepackaged cheese wedges and crackers, small foil-sealed packets of peanut butter, canned fruit, tea, and canned soft drinks.

In the hospital, Sister handed me a long gown with double ties around the waist. "Wear this isolation gown over your uniform and use disposable plastic gloves," she ordered. The gown was bulky and smelled faintly of bleach.

Then she showed me how to use a water-soluble bag for soiled linen and double-bag it. "Don't rinse out anything. The laundry staff knows how to handle it."

She called in extra cleaning help and had them wash the hospital beds, lockers, cupboards, bulkheads and deck with a disinfectant so strong that the fumes stung my nose. She had me wipe down the utility room counters with bleach and soak all the bedpans in water and bleach for twenty minutes.

I noticed that when I met passengers outside of the hospital, they shrank away from me as if I were contaminated.

The more everyone seemed to worry, the calmer Sister became. "It reminds me of working in the emergency room at Guy's Hospital in London," she said cheerfully. "I like the excitement."

Dennis Wilson, the third mate, directed thorough cleaning of the ship. Everything was washed with disinfectant. I heard him say to the crew, "I don't care how many hours we work overtime. This ship is dirty, and it has to be cleaned by the time we get into Vancouver."

At least Cece wasn't bothering me. He was too busy with the passengers crowded outside his office door, waving their tickets at him, demanding refunds in Vancouver.

The only passengers who didn't seem anxious were a newly married couple. Everyone loved them. They'd met on the trip out, married in Southampton, and were taking the return trip as their honeymoon. Through all the chaos they continued to hold hands and look into each other's eyes, seeming to be unaware of the panic around them. I watched him smooth her hair back from her forehead with a gesture so tender, my hand went to my own forehead.

As soon as I could, I made an excuse to go to the dispensary and talk to Henry Dixon. "Typhoid!" I said. "So what do you think?"

"It won't be the first time a ship has been hit by typhoid. I knew a mucker who was on the *Zena* during the Second World War, and one of the crew died of typhoid. Turned out the drinking water was contaminated with a large piece of cheese, about seven or eight pounds."

"How did it get there?"

"No one knew."

"But people wouldn't die now, would they?"

"Depends."

"On what?"

"Their general health. Their age. If what they eat or drink is contaminated, and with how much fecal material."

"Oh, Mr. Dixon!"

Fifteen minutes before I was due to go off duty, Mr. Naidoo

called for help. He was sitting bolt upright in bed, his eyes frantic. He gestured toward the kidney basin, but before I could hand it to him, he vomited blood with such force that I was covered with a warm, sodden mess of blood clots. I stood paralyzed with shock.

Sister was at the bedside immediately. With one hand, she held the kidney basin for Mr. Naidoo, and with the other, she supported his back.

"Page Dr. Connor," she ordered. "Next, go into the utility room and get out of that gown. Scrub, re-gown and get back here."

I did as I was told. Dr. Connor arrived almost immediately and hurried in to see Mr. Naidoo.

My uniform beneath the isolation gown was dry and unsoiled, but my shoes were splattered with blood. I cleaned them off with a paper towel and green soap and hurried back.

Dr. Connor had a rubber tourniquet around Mr. Naidoo's arm and was feeling for a vein. At the same time, Sister inserted a tube into Mr. Naidoo's left nostril, taped it in place and turned the oxygen gauge up to 9.

"Hang a thousand cc's," said Dr. Connor. "But run it in slowly. We don't want to blow the hole any bigger."

It was an hour before Dr. Connor said that Mr. Naidoo was out of danger. "Call me if you're the least bit concerned," he said to Sister B. on his way out.

I caught up to him as he was leaving the hospital. "I'm not sure I ever did have a typhoid shot," I said. "May I have one now, please?"

"Of course!" He looked shocked. "But why have you left it until now?"

"You said it was too late to build up an immunity if I had the shot now, remember?"

"That's true, but even so it's better to have one than not."

"And Mr. Naidoo just vomited blood all over me."

He washed his hands, prepared the vaccine and gave me the shot. Then I went to the laundry room near my cabin and piled all my clothes into a washer. I cleaned my shoes. I showered and shampooed my hair in the women's lavatory.

When I got back to my cabin, Tracey was already asleep, making soft little bubbling noises, like a water fountain.

2230 hrs. Tuesday, Jan. 13, 1970

San Francisco radioed Captain Bunyon at 1000 hrs.
confirming typhoid. Massive cleanup of ship.

146 passengers due to disembark at Vancouver, Canada, at noon tomorrow, Jan 14, 1970.

Passengers changing travel plans and radiophoning relatives.

CHAPTER SIX

A soft, insistent knocking at the door wakened me. I rolled down from the top bunk and stood close to the door. "Who is it?"

"Dennis Wilson."

I stepped out of the room, pulling my long T-shirt down even farther.

In the faint light from the lamps spaced at intervals along the passageway, Dennis's face looked even longer than usual. "Dr. Kenneth Chown, the quarantine officer in Vancouver, phoned the surgeon at midnight. Dr. Smythe told him we had ten to fifteen cases of typhoid on-board, and Dr. Chown told the captain he wanted double quarantine flags flying when we came in."

I shivered. "How soon before we get into Vancouver?"

"We should be in Vancouver in about an hour. But Anne—and this is what I came to tell you—no one is to disembark, or embark, in Vancouver until they've been given medical clearance."

Well, I'd made up my mind. I *was* leaving the ship. No

one was going to stop me.

I couldn't get back to sleep, planning how to escape the ship. Finally I got dressed and climbed the stairs to the boat deck.

The deck was slippery with frost under my feet and the air sharp in my nose. In the east, the lights of Vancouver cast an orange glow into the sky.

It was 5:30 a.m. when we sailed in under the Lions Gate Bridge. Behind the North Shore mountains, the rising sun spread a crimson stain across the sky and snowy peaks. I started shivering again, this time with eagerness to get ashore. The first thing I'd do was phone Aunt Ruth.

Back to the cabin, and after the thinness of the ocean air, the room smelled fuggy. Tracey turned over with a sigh but didn't wake up as I packed. My mouth tasted thick with night, and I remembered to pick up my toothbrush in the bathroom and shove it into my backpack. I closed the cabin door behind me with the gentlest of clicks.

As I made my way topside, I saw bags and luggage parked outside most of the cabin doors. Cabin stewards were arriving with cups of tea.

The day had lightened, and now I could see the double yellow flags flying from the masts. They must be the quarantine flags. On them were the letters *RS*. I wondered what they meant. Restricted?

By 6:00 a.m., six tugs with the words *Cates Towing* on their sterns had joined the *Ocean Spirit* and were guiding her toward the dock area. The ship had slowed so that she was barely moving.

Within minutes we were snugged into the dock, and lines

were cast off from the ship and secured. The gangway from B Deck rattled out from the side.

Land smells: roasting coffee, coconut oil and burning cinders. Land sounds: trains shunting along, a siren, the hum of early morning traffic.

Six men and a woman stood together on the pier below. All carried briefcases and looked up expectantly at the *Ocean Spirit.*

When I took the stairs down to B Deck, a crowd of passengers were milling around the gangway. Mr. Guiness and his wife were among them, pushing their way to the head of the crowd. Mrs. Guiness held a handkerchief over her nose and mouth.

The first officer stood ready to greet the visitors when they stepped off the gangway. All of the men but one wore dark business suits; that one had on a blue uniform with brass buttons. The woman's beige raincoat was brightened with a green-and-brown patterned scarf at the neck.

"I'm Dr. Kenneth Chown," said one of the men. His voice was friendly and his manner forthright. He had a strong jaw and he wore glasses with dark upper rims like wings.

"The captain is waiting to meet you in the purser's office," said the first officer. "If you'll follow me, please."

They started to walk away. I darted forth and put one foot on the gangway, set to bolt. And heard a shout.

"You, there! Stop! No one is to leave the ship." A hand clamped my shoulder. It was Cece Rathbone, and the smile on his face was smug.

The first officer and guests turned to see what the commotion was about. "I'd like to speak to the girl," Dr. Chown said to the first officer, and he walked toward me.

"Let's step aside here for a moment," he said, motioning to a spot. The blood pounded in my ears.

"You needn't be frightened of me," he said. "I'm here to help." Behind the glasses, his eyes were clear and steady. "Did you know that there is an epidemic of typhoid on-board? And that no one is to leave the ship?"

"But I have to get off," I pleaded.

"We have to keep the typhoid contained and not let it reach into the city."

"But I don't have typhoid," I said loudly. "I've only been on the ship four days."

"What is your name and where did you board?"

"Anne McLaughlin-Scott. San Francisco." I rubbed my hands nervously down the sides of my jeans, the material feeling harsh under my palms.

"McLaughlin-Scott," he said, slowly. "Not a common name. Had a classmate at McGill named Andrew McLaughlin-Scott. Went on to work on DNA—enzymes. Any connection?"

"Oh, yes!" I said quickly. "That's my dad." As soon as I'd said the words, I was sorry.

"Are you a passenger, Anne?"

"No, I've been working on-board."

"Where?"

"In the hospital. As an aide."

"You could be helpful to me."

"I don't think so."

"I'm going to run into obstacles in this investigation. You have access to the hospital, and if you're anything like your father, you'll be both observant and truthful. I need that."

I hesitated. If I did help him, I'd be able to get more and better information for Michael. And he wasn't going to let me off the ship anyway.

"What are you afraid of?" he asked gently.

"That you'll contact my father."

His forehead creased. After a moment, he said, "I guess you have your own reasons. I'll respect them. Is it a deal?"

"Okay."

"Good girl."

When I went on duty at eight that morning, Sister B. said, "Dr. Kenneth Chown is with Dr. Smythe examining the patients for transfer to a city hospital. Make sure each patient is clean and wearing a paper gown. Put their personal belongings in a plastic bag and label it with their name."

Dr. Chown and Dr. Smythe were standing beside Mr. Naidoo's bed. Dr. Smythe said, "This patient has been sick since the beginning of the trip. We thought it was the flu."

"A natural assumption," said Dr. Chown. He lay his hands on Mr. Naidoo's abdomen and pressed slightly. "But there's something here that's not quite right. Feel this."

Dr. Smythe did so.

"It will need X-raying," said Dr. Chown.

"Yes."

"Patient vomiting?"

"Not lately," said Dr. Smythe.

"He vomited blood last evening," I said, but didn't add, "all over me."

Dr. Smythe looked at me, eyebrows raised.

"There are three ambulances waiting dockside," said Dr. Chown. "Mr. Naidoo should go out on the first one." He made a note on Mr. Naidoo's chart. "Now, who's next?"

"Mrs. Aikens, a sixty-eight-year-old woman admitted during the night," said Dr. Smythe, leading the way to a two-bed ward nearby. "Her husband says she wasn't feeling well for a few days and then suddenly became confused and restless. We had to sedate her."

Mrs. Aikens's bed was near the door. Dr. Chown picked up the loose skin on her wrist. "She's dehydrated," he said, frowning. "Would you start an IV before we send her out on the ambulance? And we should have someone go with her and Mr. Naidoo."

I spoke quickly. "Could it be me?"

The doctors exchanged glances, and Dr. Smythe nodded.

"You'll come back with the ambulance, won't you, Anne?" said Dr. Chown.

"Of course."

I sat in the back of the ambulance between the two patients. Mrs. Aikens was plucking at her IV, trying to pull it out of her hand. Mr. Naidoo lay on his side, a waterproof blue pad and a kidney basin tucked under his chin.

I'd been in Vancouver before, when my family had visited Aunt Ruth on our way to Nana's in Victoria. Already I recognized the Marine Building. As the ambulance left the dock area, its siren made a few tentative whoops. I thought of all the cars that would have to pull over and stop to give us a clear path. Were there women ambulance drivers? I felt as if I were in a movie. I didn't know what to do except to hold Mrs. Aikens's hand still so that the IV needle stayed in the vein, and keep an eye on Mr. Naidoo.

All of a sudden I remembered the day, when I was four years old, that my mother was taken away in an ambulance. The red light went round and round. The tube that went down her throat was red. The basin that caught whatever came up was shiny steel and held a puddle of mucus with bits of white—like dissolved chalk. "Must have taken the whole bottle," said the ambulance driver.

"How're ya doin' back there?" called out the ambulance attendant, bringing me back to the present.

"Fine," I said. I shook my head to clear it. "Do you think I'd have time to make a couple of quick phone calls when we get to the hospital?"

"Sure. You riding back with us?"

"'Fraid so."

"Don't blame you for not wanting to go back."

"I promised someone I would." There was something about Dr. Chown that made me think of Dad and the way I used to feel about him. My dad had been ten feet tall, my hero. He always knew the right thing to say and do. I had felt so safe with him running my world.

But after Mom's trip to the hospital in the ambulance, Dad started to do whatever she said. A holiday in Hawaii? "We'll get someone in to look after Anne." Spending too much time at the lab? "I'll be home by five." Always reading scientific journals in the evening? "No, we'll go to the movies, that's fine."

I'm never going to go back home, I told myself. Never. I won't be like Dad. I won't cave in to my mother the way he did.

The siren stopped abruptly, and the ambulance slowed and turned into a hospital driveway. The back doors opened and the two patients were brought out on their stretchers and wheeled to the entrance door of the Vancouver General Hospital, Fairview Pavilion. A couple of reporters were hanging around the entrance, and flashbulbs popped.

It was an old building with an echo inside and the smell of new paint over old plaster. Nurses appeared, a doctor. One nurse took the transfer papers from the ambulance driver and pointed toward the end of the hall. "There's a nurse waiting for you," she said.

I spotted a pay phone and headed for it. The palms of my hands were wet with perspiration as I dropped in my dime and pawed through my wallet. I couldn't find the slip of paper with my aunt's phone number on it, and there was no phone book. I searched my wallet again and found the note stuck between my library card and my driver's licence.

Aunt Ruth's phone rang and rang. I let ten rings go by, then dialed again. Still no answer. Where could she be? It wasn't even nine in the morning. She wouldn't be out shopping this early. Asleep? I rang again. Nothing. I slumped against the wall. Until now, I hadn't realized how much I had been counting on her.

When I dialed the phone number Michael had given me, a

male voice answered after the first ring. He sounded guarded. "No, he's not here. No, I don't know when. Yes, I'll take a message."

"Tell him Anne phoned and that she has some notes for him. He'll have to come and get them. He'll understand."

Big fat zero. I was stuck. Even if I didn't go back to the ship, I had nowhere to stay and not that much money in my wallet. I had wages coming to me, but …

The ambulance driver walked toward me, pointing to his watch and motioning toward the ambulance. I fished around in the coin return slot and felt a stray dime, a good sign. I pocketed it and joined him.

We were back at the ship within an hour of leaving it. Dr. Chown had just finished examining the last of the patients. "They're all to go to Shaughnessy or the Vancouver General," he was saying. "Have them ready for the ambulance each time it returns so there will be no time lost." He turned and saw me, and there was relief in his smile. "Anne, would you ask Sister to have all the passengers who want to disembark here in Vancouver report to midships hospital immediately?"

When I gave the message to Sister, her lips tightened with disapproval. "What's this about you going off in one of the ambulances? You didn't even ask!"

Dr. Chown's voice behind us was firm. "I'd like to have this young woman as my assistant while I'm on the ship. Could you arrange that for me, Sister?"

Sister's face flushed red. "Well, I don't know," she blustered. "It's not up to me."

"If you would be so kind as to see to it," he said. "We'll examine the patients in the treatment room. And I'd like you to arrange to have all crew members receive a purge. We'll need a stool specimen from each one."

"Yes, Dr. Chown," said Sister.

"And each member of the crew is to have a blood test. That's all set up in the aft hospital."

"Yes, Dr. Chown."

"Come along, Anne." When we were off by ourselves, he asked, "Why so glum?"

I told him about Aunt Ruth and how I'd planned to stay with her when I did get off the ship. "She wasn't there! And if I want to phone again, well, there's a long lineup at the radio room on-board."

"Stick with me, Anne. I need to make a few calls, and they'll give me priority. Just keep the call short."

At that moment, if Dr. Chown had asked me to go to the darkest subcontinent and work with him among the pygmies, I'd have gone cheerfully.

I stayed with him while he examined the passengers who wanted to disembark, the Guinesses among them. "If you feel the least bit ill," he told each passenger, "I want you to report to the nearest public health authority."

On my way to lunch, I noticed a large crowd of passengers walking up the gangway from the dock. Some of them carried hand luggage, as if they were boarding. Dr. Chown and his colleagues had gone ashore for lunch, and as I stood there wondering what to do, I saw them get out of a taxi on the wharf. I hurried to meet them at the head of the gangway and told Dr. Chown about the passengers boarding.

"My God, who's responsible for this?" He ran up to the bridge so fast I had trouble keeping up with him. "Captain Bunyon," he shouted, "I gave strict orders that no one was to come on this ship. You have thirty minutes to get them off!"

Captain Bunyon could yell as loudly as Dr. Chown. "I did *not* give orders that anyone could board. But I will order that they be removed immediately."

We walked away, Dr. Chown still furious. "I can only hope that none of them have been on-board long enough to eat or drink anything," he fumed. "Keep your fingers crossed."

Just before lunch, Bob and another patient were transferred to the Vancouver General Hospital. His temperature had spiked again. I went in to say goodbye. "You're going to be all right," I said, taking his hand, "and as soon as I can, I'll come visit you."

"This is all about what happened at Southampton," he mumbled.

"What? What happened at Southampton?"

"Miss Scott!" Sister interrupted loudly. "When you're not on the phone, you're talking to patients. There's work to be done. The utility room is a disgrace."

When I did get away for lunch, Tracey was already eating in the crew's mess. "What a day!" she said. "They're starting to bring in the stool specimens and it smells like a shithouse back there."

"Tracey," I said, "do you know anything about what happened at Southampton?"

Her fork stopped midway to her mouth. "What *are* you going on about?"

"Bob was transferred to the Vancouver General just before lunch. Before he left, he said that this was all about what happened at Southampton."

Something flickered in her eyes, but she went back to her lunch without answering.

"Do you know anything at all about it, Tracey?" I persisted.

"I know I've got a good job, and so does my boyfriend Joe. And that's all I know, mate."

"But this is important!"

"It all depends on which side of the fence you're on."

"Tracey!"

"No, you just shove it. I'm asking Cece for a transfer to another cabin."

"But why?"

"Because I'm not a brown-noser and I don't want to bunk with one." She stood up to leave.

I tried to finish my lunch, but there was a huge lump at the back of my throat.

The afternoon was as busy as the morning. Dr. Chown had me draw a spot map showing where the sickest patients had eaten, slept and worked. Then I had to examine the crew lists to find out who had joined the ship before she sailed out of Southampton. When I handed him the report, he examined it with interest.

"All but one ate in the crew's mess," he commented. "And

look, fourteen Goanese. Typhoid's common in that part of the world. Run this note up to the captain for me, Anne, will you?" I read it quickly as I carried it to the captain.

> Please broadcast on PA system that all persons who have ever had typhoid or been in contact with a known carrier are to report to the ship's hospital immediately.

I was in the hospital when they began to trickle in, twenty-seven crew and three passengers. One was Dennis Wilson. "I thought you'd be long gone by now," he said quietly. "Weren't you going to contact your aunt?"

"She didn't answer when I phoned," I said. "I've been calling all morning on the ship-to-shore phone."

I handed Dennis a small medicine cup full of a clear yellow liquid. "Sorry to do this to you, but Dr. Chown wants a stool specimen from everyone."

He tossed it back. "Hope it doesn't work too quickly," he said. "I'm due on watch."

That afternoon Captain Bunyon and Dr. Chown had yet another row. "No way are you sailing on schedule," said Dr. Chown, thrusting his chin forward, belligerent as a bulldog.

"The World Wide Shipping agents give me my orders," the captain said, just as stubbornly.

"This ship stays in harbour," barked Dr. Chown. "If pushed, I'll invoke Article 19, subsection 1, of the Canadian quarantine regulations."

"Sir—" Captain Bunyon sputtered.

"Typhoid is a communicable disease, and I can detain this vessel for as long as necessary for disinfecting personnel, luggage and cargo."

The captain shoved his hands into his pockets and took a deep breath. "All right," he said. "I'll delay sailing for two days."

Dennis was on the bridge, and for the first time I thought I saw an expression in his eyes similar to the one I'd seen in Tracey's. *Wary.* Was he wary of me? Had I placed myself on the other side of an invisible line?

"Anne," said Dr. Chown as we walked away, "can you take me on a tour of the ship?"

"I don't know my way around all that well," I said. Some things I had learned from the diagram of the ship, and everything else I knew, Henry Dixon had told me. I wondered what he would think of my helping Dr. Chown.

"I think we have a carrier on-board," said Dr. Chown. "The disease is spreading so rapidly, I suspect it's not a food handler. It's more likely to do with the water and sewage systems."

He particularly wanted to see the galleys. "Pretty poor state of affairs," he said when I took him to the European crew's mess. "The floors are filthy. Dishes piled up. Seamen eating right in the room where the clean plates are kept."

I pointed out the sink. "We wash our cutlery there."

He grunted disapproval. "Anne, your patient, Mr. Ayub Naidoo, is to be X-rayed at the Vancouver General. I'm pretty sure he has a large stomach cancer."

"Does he have typhoid?"

"That, too."

"Is he going to die?"

"I think he has about three months left ... Don't look so sad, Anne. He'll be kept as comfortable as possible, I assure you."

I spent the rest of my shift with Dr. Chown. It was hard to keep up with him and his running commentary, but I made notes.

Before I went off duty, I went to the dispensary to see Henry Dixon. I told him everything that had happened and about being designated Dr. Chown's flunky.

"It's making it tough for me with the others," I said, thinking of Tracey and maybe Dennis. It really hurt.

His eyes were sympathetic. "Well, lass, you're stuck with it."

"I understand how they feel, but—"

"You have to do what you think is right."

2200 hrs. Wednesday, Jan. 14, 1970

8:30 a.m.: 18 patients transferred to Vancouver hospitals.

9:00 a.m.: Water samples taken by public health inspector: aft ship's hospital, bar tap in the crew's rec room, European crew's mess. Samples to be examined for coliform content, BC health department laboratories.

10:30 a.m.: 146 passengers wishing to disembark in Vancouver cleared by Dr. Chown. 900 passengers and 583 crew members remain.

11:00 a.m.: First of stool specimens from Goanese new to the crew sent to provincial lab, to be examined for typhus bacilli.

Ship's sewage holding tanks are on automatic system discharging every 1.5 hrs or when 50% full. Because tanks discharge into harbour, Dr. Chown is preparing to super-chlorinate to a residue of 50 parts per million. Liquid chlorine will be added to toilets farthest from holding tanks.

CHAPTER SEVEN

"Someone was looking for you yesterday afternoon," said Cece Rathbone when I saw him in the passageway. I was going on duty early, after wakening from a nightmare of someone chasing me down a long, torturous path.

"Who?" It had to be my family. They'd managed to track me down.

"Didn't say. Tall young man with red hair in a ponytail. Looked like a hippie to me."

"Where? When? Why didn't someone come and get me?"

"We're all busy, aren't we? You seem upset. Your boyfriend?"

"What time was this?"

"Maybe four? He asked one of the quartermasters on gangway watch if he could talk to you."

"And what did the quartermaster say?"

"That you were working. Then the chap wanted to know when you'd be off. I told him we didn't know, that you often had to work late."

"Did he say he was coming back?"

"I didn't stay around long enough to hear."

I turned and stomped off to the gangway to wait for Dr. Chown. I was furious with Cece. I was down the gangway and off the ship as soon as Dr. Chown had stepped out of the taxi. "I need to talk to you, Dr. Chown."

"Must be important," he said.

"I've got to get off the ship! You know that I need to get in touch with my aunt. Every chance I get I phone her, but she's never home. And now I'm not being called when I have visitors." I told him what had happened. "I mean, I could have talked to my visitor from the ship while he stood on the dock!"

He nodded.

"Besides," I said, "one of the crew who was sent to Vancouver General was discharged last night. He came back to the ship to pick up his gear, then he quit his job and left the ship. So why can't I?"

"I'll see what I can do," he said.

"I feel so powerless," I stormed. "Story of my life."

"You have more power than you know," he said mildly.

"Like what?"

"Like making your family sad and worried."

"All the more reason for you to let me off the ship! Then I can get in touch with Aunt Ruth. Please!"

"Anne, I've told you how important you are to me, your eyes and ears. You may not know it, but I'm being blocked on this investigation every step of the way."

"It's not easy for me, either," I argued as we reached the hospital. "My roommate moved out this morning, and people are beginning to treat me like a traitor."

Dr. Chown pushed open the door, and the night nurse hurried up to us. "The provincial lab wants you to phone them immediately," she said.

Dr. Chown went to the phone and dialed, then motioned for me to stand beside him, holding the receiver so that I could hear. He smelled of soap and mouthwash, and the collar of his starched white shirt was immaculate.

"Provincial lab, Dr. Smith speaking."

"Gordon, it's Ken Chown."

"My God, Ken, you're not going to believe this! The technician checked the water samples first thing this morning—the ones taken from the ship yesterday—and one showed a presumptive coliform content. And it's been only eighteen hours!"

Dr. Chown tensed beside me. "Where's the sample from?"

"The European crew's mess, midships. There's no doubt about it—there's a fecal contamination in the water supply."

"I've already ordered super-chlorination," said Dr. Chown.

"Ken, that will destroy the evidence. How are we going to prove that the epidemic was caused by the ship's water?"

"I know," said Dr. Chown. "And we won't be able to prove that the fecal contamination holds typhoid bacillus. But it has to be done, Gordon."

"Well, I agree. Our chief engineer's already on his way, should be there in the next fifteen minutes. Something to do with getting rid of the garbage. Apparently the head chef on the ship is on the warpath."

"I wouldn't let them take the garbage off the ship last night," said Dr. Chown. "I've arranged to have it loaded on a barge tonight, tugged out to sea and dumped on the outgoing tide."

Dr. Chown hung up and turned to me. "Up on deck with you and keep an eye peeled for the provincial health engineer. Bring him here immediately."

I ran.

"Mr. MacGregor," said Dr. Chown to the dour-faced public health engineer, "we'll need equipment that will deliver a massive dose of chlorine into the ship's water supply, five parts per million. The water will taste awful, but at least it will be safe."

"Aye," said the engineer, making notes.

Dr. Chown then announced that we were going topside to talk to the captain. Up we went, and he explained the situation to Captain Bunyon. "Please announce to all crew and passengers that they are not to drink the ship's water until the new chlorination system is working. In the meantime, I'll arrange to have containers of Vancouver water delivered to the ship for cooking and drinking."

The captain's eyes narrowed. "The ship's agent thinks you're making a mountain out of a molehill," he said.

Dr. Chown ignored him. "And I'd like you to re-broadcast the appeal to all passengers and crew to report any contact they may ever have had with any typhoid."

The captain bit down hard on his pipe.

On the way back down to the hospital, Dr. Chown said, "The Spanish liner *Madrid* was in Southampton just before the *Ocean Spirit* laid over for maintenance. Later, the *Madrid* had thirty cases of typhoid on-board. I need to find out what kind of typhoid it was, or whether this is a fresh outbreak."

"One of the crew mentioned to me that something happened in Southampton," I said.

Dr. Chown stopped and stared at me. "When was this?"

"Yesterday morning."

"Bring him to me."

"I can't. He's a patient in the Vancouver General."

"Do you think you could find out more for me?" Dr. Chown's eyes were like steel.

"If you'll let me go ashore," I bargained.

"Yes, now, immediately. I'll tell the hospital not to expect you in for the rest of the day."

"He's in the last room on the right," the unit clerk at the isolation ward told me. "But first you'll have to check with his nurse if he can have visitors."

"It's all right," I said, "I'm from the ship's hospital. You can see I've just come from there." I flipped open my parka to show her my uniform. She waved me on and went back to her paperwork.

I headed down the long hallway, passing a sign on a pedestal that read, "Grand Rounds at 9:00." I checked my watch: quarter to.

At one side of the door to Bob's room was a wagon stacked with clean linen, masks, gloves, paper and plastic bags, old newspapers carefully folded, a bottle of green soap and another of bleach. At the other side was an isolation gown hanging on a hook. I hung up my parka, put the heavy gown on over my hospital uniform, wrapped the ties round twice and tied them securely. I tapped softly at the door and opened it.

The room was small, with a view from the window of neighbourhood houses among leafless trees. Bob sat listlessly in bed, half-watching the news on TV. An anchorman was saying, "The health officer is quoted as follows: 'This is a red light to us. It means that it is highly likely that the drinking water from at least one water tap on-board the *Ocean Spirit* contains human feces.'"

I stayed at the door until the end of the report. Bob's face had turned grim, deep lines etched along each side of his nose to his mouth. The anchorman turned to news of an avalanche in the interior of BC, and Bob switched off the TV.

"What do you think?" I asked, moving from the doorway to his bed. "Do you think there's a connection with what happened at Southampton?"

His face smoothed out and became blank, like a stranger's. "Dunno."

Tension filled the space between us.

"You said you'd come," he said after a moment. "I'm glad to see you."

"I got special permission to get off the ship. I brought you a couple of magazines." I spread *Sports Illustrated* and *Mad* on his bed table. "I don't know if you're ready for these, yet," and I added a Coffee Crisp and a Jersey Milk chocolate bar to the magazines.

"Not for a while," he said. "I'm still on IV's."

"Still feeling punk?"

"Bad enough. The doctors here say I was given the wrong

antibiotic on-board ship. It should have been Chlor—Chloram—Chloramphenicol. Four grams a day. Not Tetracycline."

"Are you on the new one now?"

"Yeah. Feel a little better since they put me on it."

"I can't stay long," I said, wishing I could. "The doctors will be making rounds in a few minutes."

"A whole team of them—interns, residents, specialists. Never seen typhoid before."

"I can understand if you don't want to talk about what happened in Southampton, Bob, but it *is* important. Right now, Dr. Chown is working in the dark. Anything you could say would help."

"I *can't* talk about it."

I took a step closer. "You mean you've been *ordered* not to."

He closed his eyes. "It's that, or my job."

"And you figure we won't be seeing each other again, and that you have to make a living, and you like working for the company," I said in a rush.

A wave of red started in his neck and spread up into his face.

Voices out in the hallway came closer. "I'd better go," I said. "But please think about it, Bob. There are people on-board who could still be infected."

"They'll be all right. At least they're not out at sea."

"I guess." I groped for the right words. "But we're still friends, aren't we?" I asked.

"At least that."

On the way down the stairs, I replayed my conversation with Bob again and again, wishing I'd used a different approach, led up to it perhaps, softened him up at first. The way my mother handled my father. A way I despised. How could my father fall for it? Well, at least Bob wasn't a pushover. Wrong—he was a pushover for the cruise ship company. How was I going to tell Dr. Chown I'd come up with a blank? Then again, maybe Bob was feeling too sick to talk about it. Maybe he'd tell me another time.

I was thinking so hard that I almost bumped into Mr. and Mrs. Guiness near the Emergency entrance. "My wife woke up sick this morning," said Mr. Guiness. Mrs. Guiness did look ashen and trembly. "I'll sue the bastards," he said, breathing hard.

I caught a bus a few blocks away on Broadway, transferred to a Number 7 Dunbar and got off at 28th Avenue, two blocks from Aunt Ruth's house. It looked exactly the way I remembered it, the same small bungalow with old chestnut trees lining the boulevard. The doorbell still hadn't been repaired, and there was no response to my loud knocking at the front door.

Along the path that went around to the back, clumps of green shoots pushed through the damp earth. The branches of the pussy willow by the back steps were beaded with silver catkins.

I hammered on the back door until my knuckles were sore. "Aunt Ruth! Aunt Ruth!" I called.

An older woman's face appeared briefly at the window of

the house next door, and the next thing I knew, she was out on her back porch, a sweater pulled around her shoulders. "There's no one home," she said. She had tight white curls, bright blue eyes and pink cheeks. Her voice was strong.

"Do you know my Aunt Ruth? She didn't answer when I phoned."

"You are the second person in as many days who has come looking for her. There was an older woman here yesterday, came in a taxi."

"Tall?"

"And thin."

Nana. "What did you tell her?"

"That Ruth was out of town for a short while. Can I do anything for you, dear? You look awfully pale."

I took a couple of deep breaths.

"I've been keeping an eye on Ruth's place for her," the woman said. "She phones every week. I'll tell her you were here. What's your name, dear?"

I hesitated. Would Nana be back? "Anne," I said.

"Where can I reach you?"

I didn't know what to say.

"Wait, I'll write down my phone number for you. Why don't you phone me in a day or two?"

I ate an early lunch at a small café on West Broadway, then phoned Michael. When he answered, I felt the back of my knees soften. "I tried to get hold of you on the ship yesterday," he said. "Where are you now?"

"At a fish and chips shop." I looked out the window of the

café. "The Hollywood Theatre is just across the street."

"That's just four blocks from here," he said. The world brightened immediately.

Michael's house was three storeys high and had an old-fashioned cupola on the top. A cat draped its length over a loveseat on the verandah, jet black against the green-and-white striped covering.

A girl answered my knock. "Michael," she called loudly. "Someone here for you."

Michael came out of a room at the back. His hair, which yesterday had been red and in a ponytail, according to Cece, was brown and cut to shoulder length today. He wore bell-bottom jeans, ravelled on the bottom, sandals without socks, a ragged T-shirt and glasses with thin gold rims. The girl touched his arm briefly before leaving, a gesture so intimate I felt a twist of jealousy.

"I didn't know you wore glasses," I said awkwardly.

"I don't. These are clear lenses."

"I'd know you anywhere."

"That's not reassuring. Did you bring your notebook?"

"You're lucky, I put it in my purse when I came ashore. I'm getting so paranoid, I actually keep it hidden under my mattress."

He took me down the hall to his room, which held only a backpack and an open bedroll on the floor. "Sit down while I read this." He patted a spot beside him on the bedroll, and I sank down into it.

He opened my notebook and began to read through it quickly. "Really excellent," he said. "I'm impressed." For the first time, there was interest in his eyes when he looked at me. “It’s top of the news, you know. I won’t have any trouble selling an exclusive. But it needs photos.”

“I did take one.”

“I’d like to get on-board and take more.”

“I don’t think Dr. Chown would let you.”

“How can I get on the right side of this Dr. Chown?”

“Maybe if you found out what happened at Southampton.” I told him the details. “It’s the only reason Dr. Chown let me leave the ship today, so that I could try to get the information. I feel awful that I’ve let him down.”

“If this Bob knows, then other crew will, too. A couple of drinks and I could get them talking. I’d need to get on-board. Would you introduce me to Dr. Chown? I think I could convince him.”

“How? When?”

“Now. I’ll go back to the ship with you.”

“I don’t know, Michael.”

“Think about it. Mind if I make a few notes from your journal?”

While he made them, I walked to the window and stared out at the back lane. It seemed to me that I had always been looking out of windows.

“So, Anne, how have things been going?” Michael held out my journal to me. I walked over to get it and he pulled me down beside him.

As soon as I could breathe normally again, I said, “I’ve been having trouble reaching Aunt Ruth. I counted on being able to stay with her and get back to school. Every time I think of how far behind I'm getting, I panic."

"You could always stay here. I'll put in a word for you with the others."

"You mean that?"

"You'd have to pay rent, but it's not much. We share the kitchen, bathroom and phone."

"I could get a part-time job. Oh, Michael, do you really think I could?" I hugged him in gratitude.

He made a funny noise, and the next thing I knew, I was lying beside him on the bedroll and he was leaning over me, stroking my forearm, from my wrist up to the front of the elbow and back down again. Every cell in my body responded. His hand moved to my neck.

"Hey, Mike!" shouted a male voice. "Chuck is at the front door. Something about Nelson."

"Be right there," Michael called, rolling back. "Paperwork," he said. "Look, while I'm dealing with that, could you sketch out the layout of the ship?"

"I'll try."

He handed me the notes he'd made, and I began to rough out the deck plans as best I could.

"Have you thought about it?" he asked, rummaging through his backpack for a large manila envelope.

"About what?"

"Asking Dr. Chown."

"Yeah. I will."

"I'll come down to the dock to see you at about four. Is that enough time?"

"I think so."

"Mark your cabin on the map so I can find you if I have to."

"They won't let you on-board," I warned.

"We'll see," he said.

I made an *X* for my cabin.

Dr. Chown shook his head when I passed on Michael's request to come aboard. "As if I'm not in enough hot water," he said. "If this young man can find out anything about Southampton, well, we'll see."

Michael turned up at the dock at four. I went to the railing and shouted down, "Sorry, he said no."

"Not to worry," he called back cheerfully. "Keep up the good work. I'll be in touch in a few days."

I spent the rest of the day handing out laxatives. Thirty-two passengers and crew had answered the captain's call for those who had been in contact with typhoid at any time during their lives.

"Anyone can be a carrier," Dr. Chown explained to an elderly man who had once worked in a slaughterhouse with a man later diagnosed with typhoid. "Some carriers never show the disease, or give it to other people, but there can be a breakdown of personal hygiene as one gets older …"

The man was outraged. "Just because I'm eighty, doesn't mean I'm senile!" he spluttered.

"There was no slight intended," Dr. Chown said. "I was speaking in general terms. It can happen with anyone at any age. That's why people on a typhoid register are never allowed to handle food."

Before going to bed that night, I went up on deck. The rain that had been threatening all day was now a deluge, so heavy that at first I thought it was a trick of the rain and the light at the aft gangway that made it look like a man's shadow lurked there. For a moment the shadow became a person, silhouetted against one of the deck lights. It looked like Michael.

I went to my cabin. If it was Michael, there would soon be a knock at my door. Tracey had moved everything out, and when I saw that she hadn't even left a note, I felt gutted. The room was empty and lonely.

But Michael never came to my cabin that night. I told myself it couldn't have been Michael I'd seen slip up onto the ship.

CHAPTER EIGHT

Soon after breakfast, passengers began to arrive at the hospital with their stool specimen bottles wrapped discreetly in paper bags or sealed in envelopes. They offered these, eyes averted, as if the specimens didn't belong to them. By late morning we had hundreds of specimens, from both passengers and crew, boxed and ready to be taken to the provincial lab.

"Anne, could you find a dolly and take these to my car?" Dr. Chown said.

"Your car? I thought you always took a cab."

"Not today. I've had taxi drivers turn me down before when I've tried transporting stool specimens. And I'd like you to come with me," he added. "I'll need your help at the other end."

I loaded the samples and we took them across the Granville Street Bridge to the provincial lab, a beige concrete-and-steel building adjacent to the Vancouver General Hospital. When I went inside to get a dolly to unload, the smell of feces rose up like a warm brown wave.

"Do you ever get used to the smell?" I asked a woman behind the counter. "Not really," she said. "Fridays are the worst. That's the day all the stool specimens from across the province come in."

I borrowed the dolly, and Dr. Chown and I loaded the specimens into the elevator and took them up to the next floor. Everyone we met greeted Dr. Chown with respect, in sharp contrast to his treatment on-board ship. There, the hostility was barely suppressed. He even walked differently here, his step buoyant and his head thrown back as he gave a friendly greeting to everyone.

The director of the provincial laboratory was in his office. I remembered him from the day the *Ocean Spirit* had arrived and been placed under quarantine. "Anne, this is Dr. Gordon Smith. Gordon, Anne. Anne works in the midships hospital and has been kind enough to assist me."

Dr. Smith nodded in my direction and turned quickly back to Dr. Chown, excitement spilling forth with his words. "It's confirmed that there was, or has been, fecal matter in the water sample from the European crew's mess. The coliform count of samples from the ice-water tap in the first-class galley was 5.1 per 100 millilitres, high enough to be called 'doubtful.' This needs investigation," he said, rubbing his hands.

I pulled out my notebook and tried to record the main points of what he'd said.

Dr. Smith hardly stopped for breath. "No doubt the superchlorination has wiped that out now. And here's something. The provisional results of the stool specimens from several crew members are positive for typhoid bacilli." He handed the report to Dr. Chown.

Dr. Chown took his time reading it. "None of these men

has shown any symptoms," he said.

"Then perhaps we've found our carrier." Dr. Smith's tone was jubilant. "Ah," he said, "here's MacGregor, just the man we want."

"I have the information you wanted, Dr. Chown, about the mechanics of the ship," said Mr. MacGregor. "She has twenty-four supply tanks that can hold 2,300 tons of water. In addition, there are seven tanks below the bilges in the ship's engine room. Four of those are used from time to time, when needed."

"I've cabled the Central Enteric Laboratories in London to ask what type of typhoid had been discovered aboard the Spanish liner *Madrid*," said Dr. Chown. "Yesterday I learned that the *Ocean Spirit* crew hospitalized in San Francisco have K1. It's a type indigenous to the Indian subcontinent, and I'm betting that our carrier is the Goanese steward who showed a positive stool specimen but no sign of the disease."

"Any other positives?" asked Mr. MacGregor.

"One from a European who has never been to India. But listen to this: the Goanese steward's medical records show that he was on another World Wide ship last October, became ill and was hospitalized in Cape Town. He was discharged from the hospital when the *Ocean Spirit* was in Cape Town, and promptly signed on the ship."

"Since we've already had one positive water sample from the European crew's mess, I'll order six more," said Mr. MacGregor. "Plus one from the ice-water tap in the first-class galley. That's the tap the engineers use to fill their water jugs, and they account for most of the cases of typhoid. Another thing—the dishwashing procedure needs to be changed to ensure a two-minute soak in scalding water."

"I agree," said Dr. Chown. "I'll order that a disinfectant be added to the final rinse."

We left Dr. Smith's office, and I followed Dr. Chown from lab to boardroom and then upstairs to yet another lab. Everyone was dressed in white lab coats. I watched the meticulous labelling of specimens, the making of smears on slides from cultures, the examining of slides under microscopes, the careful recording of data. The smell was stronger here. I found myself taking shallow breaths.

At last Dr. Chown was ready to leave. "I need to stop back at my apartment to pick up some papers," he said to me. "I'll make us a bite of lunch before we go back to the ship."

He lived on the top floor of a large apartment building overlooking English Bay. Five freighters lay at anchor across Burrard Inlet, off Point Grey, their bows swinging with the outgoing tide toward Georgia Strait. Stanley Park lay to the north of the apartment, and shafts of sunlight lit up its cedar trees.

Dr. Chown put Debussy on the stereo before pushing through swinging doors to the kitchen. Soon the smell of cooking green pepper and onion came drifting into the dining area, where I stood looking at a painting. It showed a smooth-planed totem pole in the left foreground, and behind and to the right, yellow cats' eyes glittered out of massed foliage. The signature in the bottom right corner was "E. Carr."

Dr. Chown served omelettes and French bread. He had

a glass of Pommard. "Too bad you're underage," he said. It wasn't until we poured coffee that he became serious.

"Your father phoned me last night," he said.

I spluttered coffee. "What?!"

"He saw a picture of you on the front page of the *Examiner*. You were at the side of an ambulance that was unloading patients at a hospital. He didn't know whether you were involved or just a bystander. He read the article, recognized my name and thought I might help him locate his missing daughter."

My mouth was so dry, the words seemed to stick. "What did you tell him?"

"That I would make inquiries and phone him as soon as possible. What do you want me to tell him?"

"That you couldn't find me."

"I can't lie, Anne."

"It won't be a lie. Because I'm not going back to the ship." I stood up abruptly and was at the door in seconds.

"Come back. Sit down," he said wearily. "I won't phone him."

I didn't move.

"Don't be hasty, Anne. You need to think this through."

He stood up and I put my hand on the doorknob and turned it, ready to bolt.

He took a step back. "Your father talked about private detectives. Why don't you let me try to handle him?"

"How?"

"I'll tell him that you're all right. That he needs to give you some time, some breathing space. I know he'll listen to me."

I kept my hand on the doorknob. "I want at least a month."

He took off his glasses and wiped them on the end of his tie. "You drive a hard bargain, Anne. All right. Now come back and finish your coffee."

At six that evening, eight more people suspected of having typhoid were transferred to Vancouver General Hospital. I wanted to go with the ambulance, hoping I could phone Michael and Aunt Ruth's neighbour. And I wanted to see Bob again. He might have decided to tell me about Southampton. But Sister B. flatly refused, and I didn't think Dr. Chown would let me go, either.

An hour later, tugs pulled the *Ocean Spirit* away from the dock and the crew anchored her off. Her berth was needed by another World Wide liner, the *Ocean Wind*, en route to Honolulu with nine hundred passengers aboard, all of them expecting to disembark in Vancouver.

Captain Bunyon decided to hold an all-class cocktail party that evening. When I went off duty just after eight and passed the main lounge, I could hear the clink of glasses and smell the cigar and cigarette smoke.

I changed and went to the party, too, but I felt isolated and even disliked because of my association with Dr. Chown. I wished with all my heart that I could get off the ship and get back to school, any school. It seemed that my whole life had come to a screeching halt.

It was too depressing to stay at the party. I slipped away, went to my cabin and pulled out my journal.

I was just finishing off my notes when Tracey dropped by to retrieve a murder mystery she'd left behind. She hovered at the door for a minute. Finally she said, "You all right, then?"

"I guess so."

"Cece Rathbone still sniffing around?"

"A couple of times, after he found out I was here on my own."

"Tell him straight that you'll report him to the captain."

"Oh, sure."

"Do it, Anne. Just the threat will shrivel his pecker."

"Miss you, Tracey."

"Yeah, well … All you have to do is stop brown-nosing."

At about midnight, unable to sleep, I went to the upper deck and got there just in time to see Dr. Chown leave the ship by launch. I hung over the rail and watched him go. The city lights lay beyond, out of my reach. And Michael. I'd never felt so lonely in my life.

A presence loomed out of the night and stood beside me. It was Dennis.

"I thought it was you," he said. "Haven't seen you for a few days."

"So much has been going on."

"Including my birthday," he said glumly. "Today. No mail got through from home, and I can't use the phone for a personal call. If I were home right now, someone would be buying a round at the pub to help celebrate."

"I guess you missed the cocktail party."

"No, I made a brief appearance—captain's orders. But I didn't have anything to drink because I was going on watch."

"How about right now?"

"You mean a drink? Us?"

"In your cabin. Why not?" Was I really saying this?

His cabin was close by: single, neat, with photos of his family and dog everywhere. A half-written letter lay on his desk.

"Would you like a Coke?" he asked.

I was sick of soft drinks. Everyone else on the ship drank alcohol. Sometimes it seemed that was all they did when they were off duty. "No, I'll have what you're having."

He poured himself a gin and tonic and about half the amount in another glass for me. I took a tentative sip. I liked the juniper taste of the gin.

Dennis tossed his off and poured another. "The old man is fit to be tied about the headlines in the paper today—Floating Typhoid Bomb. Some of the passengers from first class formed a committee. They met with the captain and told him they want to be kept better informed."

"What did he say?" A pleasant buzz had begun behind my eyes.

"He told them not to believe anything until it's official."

"Sounds right." I took another swallow.

"He takes it out on us, though. He said things to me tonight that—well, no man has the right to say to another man." His face had become flushed and gleamed with perspiration. "On my birthday, too." He loosened his collar and flopped onto his bunk.

My lips tingled, and a warmth spread through me that made me want to embrace the whole world, including Dennis. I reached out my hand to smooth the hair off his forehead, and he pulled me down beside him. He fumbled at my bra, and when he'd worked that off, he lay his head between my breasts. A minute later his breathing grew slow and regular. He was asleep. I looked down at his face. It seemed so young and vulnerable.

Then I noticed a leather-bound notebook lying on his night table. Did he keep a journal, too? The longer I looked at it, the more I wanted to read it. But it was his, private. I wouldn't like anyone snooping in my journal. Still—it might have important information in it.

I eased my way out from under his head, rolled off the bunk and opened the book. It seemed to be a log he was keeping. I tried to remember when the ship had sailed from Southampton. Tracey had said something about being at sea at Christmas. I flipped back to December. There it was!

> December 13, Southampton. Joined ship early. No one else aboard except for the Goanese who have no other place to stay, and a skeleton crew and dockworkers doing maintenance work. The engineers repaired the sewage storage tank in the shaft tunnel, and there was an accident—a major flooding of sewage into the tunnels.

Dennis sighed behind me. I replaced his logbook and turned to look at him. He lay on his back, his mouth open. He began to snore gently.

I stepped to the door, opened it, looked out and went below to my own cabin.

Sewage. Accident. Water contamination. Was this the connection Dr. Chown was looking for?

CHAPTER NINE

I fell into a deep sleep but woke at 4:00 a.m. with a queasy stomach, a dry mouth and a sick feeling of guilt. Everyone else on the ship drank all the time and handled it all right. There must be a knack, something I hadn't learned yet.

Henry Dixon's words came floating back into my mind, "If I stay with the ship, I run the risk of ending up either an alcoholic or a sex maniac." Did that mean sex was next for me? It was happening all around. When I went by a cabin door—it didn't matter what time of day or night—I heard rhythmic sounds, small cries, deep sighs. By the time I reached my own cabin, I would feel a sweet twist inside.

Sex was in the music I heard from the ship's lounge, in the energy between couples at tables as they leaned toward each other and touched. Sometimes I had to go up on deck and walk and walk in the cold, wet wind until I was exhausted.

I wanted to know about sex. *But not yet, not yet.* I thought about Michael. Would I go on the pill for him? Dad worked for the company that produced the pill. He said, "We don't know what the dosage of hormone should be. It's scatter-gunning. No wonder women are having adverse reactions. As for the long term effects, who knows?"

I wondered if Michael felt anything for me. There was that moment when I had visited him at his house. What if we had not been interrupted? If I went with him to Nelson, would I go to school? Or would I live in a commune and bake whole-grain bread? If he stayed in Vancouver, I could live with Aunt Ruth. Michael and I could be boyfriend and girl-friend. I'd need to go on the pill, and Aunt Ruth would know all about it.

I punched my pillow. Never mind about the pill—the most important thing was to get back to school.

So thirsty. I shouldn't have had that gin. I had a headache, too. Okay, no more drinking, at least while I'm on the ship.

When I saw Dr. Chown in the hospital at eight that morning, he looked as tired as I felt. "I've been up all night with phone calls from newspapers and agencies from around the world," he said. "I didn't dare stop answering in case it was important."

"Dr. Chown, I have something to tell you."

He seemed not to hear me. "London phoned with the news that the typhoid aboard the *Madrid*, the ship tied up along-side the *Ocean Spirit* in Southampton, was not the Asiatic K1 strain. So we can eliminate that source."

"I know what happened at Southampton."

He stopped. I had his attention now.

"The shipyard workers were repairing the sewage storage

tank, and there was an accidental major flooding of sewage into the tunnel." I looked for his reaction. It was as if a light had gone on behind his face.

"How did you learn this?"

"I snooped."

"Do you think the source is reliable?"

"Yes."

"I want to see this tunnel. I have a break around ten this morning. Come and find me wherever I am, and we'll nip down there for a quick look."

When we reached the hospital, Sister's eyes were bright with excitement. "We don't have one empty bed," she said. "I hope this is the peak of the epidemic."

"Sister, I want every member of the crew to receive a dose of cholagogue," Dr. Chown said. "It causes the gall bladder to contract and empty. If there are any typhoid bacilli there, they'll be flushed out and show up in the feces. And I want a white blood count done on all those with positive stool specimens, also those who have been in contact with known typhoid cases. We might just isolate the carrier."

By ten that morning, the nineteen new cases of typhoid—sixteen crew and three passengers—had been transferred by launch and ambulance to the city hospital. I told Sister that Dr. Chown wanted me to accompany him down to the engine rooms. Her mouth turned down like she'd swallowed vinegar, but she let me go.

I went looking for Dr. Chown, first at the crew's surgery. There Henry Dixon and Dr. Connor were trying to persuade two Indian crew members to let them draw blood from their arms.

"You see how it is," Dr. Connor was saying to Henry. "They don't like giving blood samples." The lime scent of his aftershave was particularly strong. He threw down his tourniquet. "Here, you do what you can, Henry. I'm going to take a break."

Henry began a long, soothing discourse with the crew member. "Come on, old boy," he said to the older Indian. "Sit you down." He placed one hand on the man's shoulder and pressed gently, sliding a chair under him with one foot.

The old man sat, and Henry had the tourniquet on and the blood withdrawn before the man could protest. Henry then smiled broadly at the second man and repeated the manoeuvre successfully. Both men left the room at once, muttering what sounded like threats.

Henry turned to me. "You next, lass?"

"Not this time, thanks, Mr. Dixon."

"Haven't seen you for a bit. How're you doing?"

"Okay. I have a question, though."

"You usually do."

"Why is Tetracycline still being used instead of Chloramphenicol?"

He looked at me in mock astonishment. "Who d'you think you are?"

"Someone who wants to know." I told him what Bob Miller had said, that the doctors at Vancouver General told him Chloramphenicol was the specific drug for typhoid. "Yet this morning in the ship's hospital, Dr. Connor's giving the new cases Tetracycline."

Henry shook his head. "It's not that I haven't tried. I think the good doctor forgets."

"He's too young to be forgetful."

"Young or not, he has to hold his first glass of gin in the morning with two hands," said Henry. "It's only after the second or third that he appears normal."

"Dr. Connor? He's so nice. And I've never smelled anything on him. Except maybe aftershave."

"Once, I was with him in his cabin, having a drink. Warm evening, both portholes open. I saw the masthead lights of a tug go by slowly, first past one port, then past the other. Then the tug gave two almighty blasts on her foghorn. Blah-blah! Connor jumps from his chair, lunges for the phone, picks it up and says, 'Hello? Ish Dr. Connor shpeaking.' He's tipsy, right?"

I was shocked.

"He's still an excellent doctor," said Henry.

"I suppose," I said.

"I'll have a word with Sister. She mother-hens him. But I'm surprised she didn't pick up on the Tetracycline—she usually does."

I found Dr. Chown in the aft hospital, talking to the chief public health officer of Vancouver, a stout, balding man with a flash of gold in his mouth when he spoke. "The water samples taken from the sink in the crew's mess where they wash their cutlery show a high fecal coliform content, in spite of the super-chlorination. I think it's because the crew's washrooms don't have towels. Any crew member with a gastroenteric disorder goes to the toilet frequently, and it's unlikely he'll go to his cabin for his towel, and so he probably skips the hand washing."

Dr. Chown opened his mouth to say something, but the health officer kept right on talking. "The crew member still eats three times a day and washes his cutlery by dipping it and his hands into water that others use for washing their cutlery. Bacteria from his hands and under his nails, perhaps left over from his visit to the washroom, enter the water and thus contaminate others' utensils."

Dr. Chown held up his hand. "I'll order that buckets of disinfectant be placed in the washrooms and that all crew members must dip their hands into it after using the lavs. I'll order another bucket for the crew's mess with instructions to leave cutlery there to soak."

I caught Dr. Chown's eye. "Excuse me," he said to the health officer. "I've got a lead to investigate."

The engine rooms were located on H Deck, below the water line. In a side passageway, Dr. Chown and I came to a narrow doorway and looked down into what seemed to be the very bowels of the ship.

Dr. Chown went first, down the ladder, which was almost vertical. He placed both hands on the rails, his back to the rungs, and with arms held stiff and feet barely touching the rungs, he slid down. Both heels hit the steel deck with a sharp bump. I followed.

The boiler rooms were clean, painted white and well lit.

They were two decks high and were separated from each other by watertight doors. "For safety reasons," Dr. Chown explained. The actual burners were at the bottoms of the boilers. Scoured steelwork and polished brass gleamed. The pipes and valves had been painted different colours. "A colour code of what the pipes carry," Dr. Chown said. "Salt water, fresh water, boiler feed water, condenser water, lubricating oil, hydraulic oil, fuel oil, steam." Huge insulated pipes loomed overhead. "The drainage holes in the deck feed to the bilge below," said Dr. Chown.

Although the turbines were idle, an electrical hum came from the auxiliary machinery—generators, air conditioning and refrigeration units. Dr. Chown whipped out his handkerchief and mopped his forehead. "Hot in here! Must be from the boilers. They say the steam is seven hundred degrees Fahrenheit."

"The boilers are seamless hollow forged steel," I said, and was immediately sorry. I had read this fact in one of the ship's brochures, but it sounded as if I were showing off, just the way my mother said I did.

The room smelled of hot metal, oil and cleaning solvents. And something else—something familiar, like bleach.

When I saw the turbines, I stopped in amazement. They were like the turbines on a jet plane.

We stood now in the shaft tunnels, which ran from the engine rooms to the propellers, and there was barely enough room to walk upright. "Mind your head," said Dr. Chown.

"That must be the sewage storage tank in question," Dr. Chown said, pointing to a welded steel rectangular box about four by ten feet and six feet high—about the size of a dumpster—that stood in the middle. "There'll be four or five of these, connected by pipes, to take the waste from the ship's toilets."

He was silent for a moment, then said, "You know, I'm sure I smelled chlorine when we passed through the engine room."

"As in chlorine bleach? So did I."

"Let's go back and investigate."

We returned to the engine room, where he sniffed until he found it. "Yes, here it is. And I'm pretty sure the number seven water tanks are located below here, under the bilge. The crew must have scattered chlorine on their own initiative."

"Too bad we can't ask someone," I said. The place was deserted.

"Is there anyone here?" Dr. Chown called out in a loud voice.

A burly engineer in a white boiler suit appeared after a few seconds. "What's up?" he said curtly.

"Someone has put chlorine here. Why?"

"I couldn't say."

"You must have some idea, man!"

"I believe bleach was applied at Southampton."

"Who knows about it? Captain Bunyon?"

"Maybe not. He didn't join the ship until the day before she sailed."

Dr. Chown left in such a hurry that I had to run to catch up to him. He headed straight for the bridge and burst into the wheelhouse.

"Captain Bunyon, I want to know what happened in Southampton," he demanded. "I know there was an incident, and I know that it is connected with this epidemic."

"Give me permission to go ashore, and I'll phone London," said the captain.

"Granted. And when you find out, I'll be in the midships hospital."

Dr. Chown grumbled all the way down to the hospital. "Some of the medical officials from World Wide were at me only this morning, saying that I was being too hard on the *Ocean Spirit*! Well, finally I have the captain taking me seriously. He's got something on-board that he can't handle."

Two hours later, the captain came looking for Dr. Chown. "London reports that there was an accident in the sewage tank, with major flooding of sewage into the shaft tunnels," he said through tight lips. "I don't know all the details."

After he left, Dr. Chown said, "Well, that confirms your source's information. It was brave of the captain to tell me—he is putting the welfare of his passengers and crew ahead of his employer. We'll have another look-see tomorrow. Do you happen to own a camera?"

"Yes."

"I think it's time we took some photos."

CHAPTER TEN

"You're looking a bit peaked, Anne," said Dr. Chown first thing the next morning.

"I am tired," I admitted. I hadn't felt myself since I'd had the gin with Dennis. I was beginning to wonder if I was allergic to alcohol.

"You need a day off. Twelve-hour shifts are too long for a sixteen-year-old who's still growing."

"I can't see Sister agreeing."

"I'll talk to her."

"But what about the photos?"

"We'll do that now and get it out of the way."

I went back to my cabin for the camera and an extra roll of film. Then we went down to the boiler and engine rooms. Yesterday everything had been quiet, but today the whole area was bustling and had a lovely smell of hot oil and steam. Stokers lit up boilers. Engineers checked lubricators. The men worked silently and efficiently, but with an air of tension.

Bob Miller had once told me that the turbines were designed to drive the ship at 22 knots. At the time I was more interested in his smile than in nautical miles, but when he'd mentioned that the engine ran at 42,500 horsepower, it got my attention.

"What's up?" I asked one of the stokers now. I recognized him as one of Bob's cabinmates, who had stayed friendly with me because of Bob.

"The old man is taking the ship up Howe Sound in a couple of hours. Bit of a break for the passengers. They're bored out of their skulls." He wiped his hands on a rag.

"I noticed," I said. "They sit around as if they were half-dead."

"So how's Bob doing? You ever hear?"

"Dr. Chown says he's off IV's and eating a soft diet."

Dr. Chown called to me. "We'll want a picture of this," he said, pointing to the ice-water tap. "The engineers drink from it, and they're the ones hardest hit."

I took two pictures while Dr. Chown veered off to chat with a junior officer. "That was some incident at Southampton," Dr. Chown said to the officer. "The captain was telling me about it yesterday."

"A bloody catastrophe is what it was."

"Were you there when it happened?"

"I was."

"That so?" said Dr. Chown mildly.

"We were tied up at the wharf in Southampton, and the dock workers were repairing the sewage tank. The pumping mechanism had been shut down, and some dockyard matey must have done something to the tank system. The sewage was released and just poured out. It flooded the tunnel."

"My God!" said Dr. Chown. "What did you do?"

"We washed it out with seawater. But the watertight door—the one that separates the tunnel from the bilge—was open. Some of the seawater and sewage flooded over to the bilge area."

I saw a pulse begin to beat in Dr. Chown's neck, just beneath the angle of his jaw. "Aren't the number seven water tanks in the double bottom under the bilge?"

"Yes. And the hatches were off some of the tanks."

"I suppose the watertight door allowing access to the bilge was open to allow the workers to pass to and fro?"

The junior officer nodded.

Dr. Chown's gaze sharpened. His voice became deadly calm. "So polluted water slopped over the tanks, the same tanks that supplement the ship's supply in the twenty-four normal fresh-water tanks."

The officer blinked rapidly and his Adam's apple bobbed up and down in his throat. "Yes," he said faintly.

"Must have been a fair amount of sewage," said Dr. Chown in a tone of confidentiality.

"Yes, it was up to here," said the junior officer, holding his hand mid-thigh.

I had my camera up and the picture taken before his hand dropped.

As we left the engine room, Dr. Chown looked triumphant. "Finally I might have proof that the water is contaminated," he said. "I'll have the number seven tanks pumped dry immediately."

He asked me to take photos of the dishwashing sinks in

the European crew's mess and the hand-washing signs posted in the lavatories. "Photograph anything else you find interesting, Anne."

"I heard that one of the ten-man cabins has a sign, 'Six down and four to go.'"

"Macabre sense of humour," Dr. Chown smiled. "But it will liven up the meeting I'm having with the shipping company officials tomorrow morning."

When I'd shot the whole roll, I took it to Henry Dixon and asked whether he could develop it for Dr. Chown before he left that day.

"Well, luv, I usually like to wait until it's dark before processing. But if Dr. Chown's in a hurry, I'll black out the dispensary. What pictures do you have that are so important?"

"The engine room, mostly. There was a sewage spill there, but I guess you already know that."

"I'd heard rumours, but I wasn't on-board at the time."

Had I said too much? "I loved the turbines," I said.

"Did you, lass? I have a picture here you might like to see." He went to his bookshelf, pulled out an oversized volume and riffled through the pages until he came to the photograph he wanted. "This is a turbine minus its outer casing," he said, pointing.

It looked like a picture of four gigantic sunbursts lined up, each one bigger than the last. "They're beautiful," I said.

"These are the steam glands fitted to each end of a turbine," he said, pointing.

"Imagine being able to understand how all this works!"

"It's multi-stage. The exhaust from the smallest goes into

the next one with its bigger blades, at lower pressure, and so on. Then the exhaust passes back to the condensers and back to the boilers."

I'd never know as much as Henry Dixon, not in a million years. But I wanted to try. I couldn't wait to go back to school and get started.

As I walked back to my cabin, already anticipating the luxury of going back to bed on my day off, I felt rather than heard the vibrations as the engines started up. It was as if the ship were coming alive and trembling with eagerness to break away.

I turned down the passageway to my cabin in time to see Dennis bend over and slide something white under my door. He straightened without seeing me and walked rapidly away.

It was a note. "Dear Anne, There's a dance this evening. Would you like to go? I hope so. I'll call for you at seven. Dennis."

I had nothing to wear but jeans. Bed would have to wait. The small boutique on C Deck was having a sale. I had some cash, not much. Maybe I could collect my wages for the week. I went to Cece Rathbone's office.

His smile vanished when I asked him for the money. "A sub against your wages? Not a chance. You'll be paid at the end of the trip, the same as everyone else. If you wanted it any different, you should have told me when you signed on."

"I thought we could get an advance in each new port," I said.

"Who's been feeding you that line of malarkey?"

I couldn't remember. I stood there, feeling like an idiot. I didn't even know how much was owed me. I'd asked Tracey once what the pay was, and she'd said, "Minimum. Fifty pounds a month—about $160."

"But I do have something for you," Cece said, opening a drawer.

It was my seaman's book, a little bigger than my passport and with a similar blue cover. Written in it were the date I had joined the *Ocean Spirit* and my position, utility steward. As I held it, I had a sense of pride.

"I still think I should get some pay," I said, my voice sounding louder than I'd intended. "I've worked twelve hours a day for seven days."

"And you've had three meals a day and a cabin to yourself, not to mention a little something on the side with one of the officers."

"You creep," I said. What could he do? Fire me?

No advance. I'd have to manage with what I had.

In the boutique I bought a fitted halter-top dress made of a shimmering fabric that looked like a fish spinning in the sunlight. It had a zipper down the front. "You can be demure or not, as suits the occasion," said the clerk. "And it's 75 percent off the original price." It was still pricey, but I could do it, and it fit perfectly.

"I'm not sure," I said, turning so that I could see all views of the dress in the mirror. My mother would have a fit if she could see how low the dress dipped in the back. "I'll need sandals."

"You look like a size eight."

"'Fraid so." My mother never let me forget it. She wore a

5A. "Your feet, Anne," she'd say. "Like your nose."

"I've got an eight in a sandal, and it's not moving," the sales clerk said. "I'll throw them in if you like them. We'll be restocking in Australia, if we ever get there."

I couldn't believe my luck. The sandals were strappy, bone-coloured and made in Italy.

Back in my cabin, I hung the shining dress on a hanger. The motion of the ship caused it to sway, as if it were already dancing.

The ship shuddered and groaned as it picked up speed, and I hurried up on deck to hang over the rail. The snowline was halfway down the mountains, and I could see the chairlift on top of Grouse Mountain. Aunt Ruth had taken me skiing there one Christmas. Where was Aunt Ruth now? Maybe she was back from her trip, and her next-door neighbour was telling her about my visit.

The ship gave a deep, three-toned blast on the siren as we passed under the Lions Gate Bridge. Once we were clear of the bridge, the *Ocean Spirit* increased its speed even more, and by the time we were off Point Atkinson, heading into the Georgia Strait, we seemed to be flying.

All thoughts of family and school dropped away into the jade green water below. How could I ever leave this ship? I was in love with it and just wanted to keep going and going.

The water was rough between the far ends of Bowen and Gambier islands, a long stretch of water called Queen Charlotte Channel according to the chart on the bulletin board. The tide was running one way and the wind blowing the other. A tug went by, pulling a raft of logs.

It was cold on deck, and I shivered. I went below to my cabin, crawled into my bunk and fell asleep watching wooded islands pass by my porthole.

I slept, I ate, I slept. I caught up with my journal entries. By dusk, the *Ocean Spirit* was back in Vancouver, tying up at the CPR dock. The city lights sparkled in the frosty air.

I showered and shampooed my hair and was doing my nails when Tracey popped by. "I hear you're going to the dance with Dennis," she said with a friendly smile.

"Who told you that?"

"You can't keep a secret on-board, mate. That's the way it is."

"And now, suddenly, I'm all right?" I still felt hurt and angry that she'd cut me off.

"Well, the captain spilled the beans about Southampton."

"That makes the difference?"

"Of course," she said cheerfully. "Do you want me to French-braid your hair? It will make you look years older."

She was right. When she'd finished, I looked at least twenty.

Right after dinner, I hurried to the dispensary to check on the film. "See here, luv," Henry said, spreading the prints out on the counter. "They're all right. You'll find the negatives in the smaller envelope."

"Thanks a million. I'll get them to Dr. Chown right away."

"You're all dolled up, lass."

"Yes."

"It's none of my business, I know, but …"

"But what?"

"If I can suggest something, luv. Don't rush. You've got plenty of time." His tone changed and he grinned. "Now get out and enjoy yourself."

Dennis called for me at seven. His first words were, "You look beautiful!" I had the front zipper down two inches below my mother's approved zone, but Dennis was looking at my face.

We went up to the dance space on B Deck, in a room enclosed by sliding glazed screens. Even with my oversized feet I felt like Cinderella, to be here with Dennis looking so handsome in his officer's uniform.

A small band of bass, piano and alto sax played the opening bars of "Stardust," and Dennis swept me out onto the parquet floor. "You really can dance!" I said admiringly.

"I took ballroom dancing at the Nautical College in London. We had a choice between that or judo."

For the first time, I was glad that my mother had made me go to dancing school. I'd hated spending Saturday afternoons learning to waltz, foxtrot, two-step, tango, samba and jive. But now it was paying off. Dennis and I found our rhythm together and soon the other couples dropped back to watch us. Even the band perked up. The more I danced with Dennis, the more I liked him. When he said, "I'm due on watch in fifteen minutes," I hated the evening to end.

It couldn't have been ten minutes after Dennis had dropped me off at my cabin door—with a goodnight kiss that left me dizzy and wanting more—that I heard a quick rap and a turning of the doorknob.

I was at the door in a flash. "Who is it?" I asked, without opening the door.

"Michael."

Michael? For a moment, I couldn't think who that was. The ship, Dennis—I'd forgotten all about the outside world.

I unlocked the door and Michael slipped in. Dressed in a black turtleneck sweater and dark work pants, he could have passed for a deckhand. He needed a shave and smelled of marijuana.

"What are you doing here?" I asked.

"Do you have any more information for me? I have to finish that article. I need the cash."

"You mean my journal?" I'd been adding to my notes, but now I realized that it had really been more for me than for Michael.

"I came aboard a few evenings ago, but I was spotted and had to leave in a hurry." He seemed jittery, shifting from foot to foot and glancing around nervously.

"I thought I saw you."

"I wanted to dig up the story of the Southampton incident, but no such luck." His eyes darted around the cabin.

"Dr. Chown got the whole story today. I've written it in the journal."

He grabbed my arm in his excitement. "Let me see it!"

I took my journal out from under my mattress and handed it to him. "Two things I haven't written in yet. One, the first tests done on the number seven water tanks were negative. Second, someone in West Vancouver wrote to the city health department complaining that they found garbage from the

Ocean Spirit washed up on the beach—including stool samples in plastic bags."

"I'll make notes," Michael said, pulling a notepad and pen out of his back pocket.

"You can use my desk."

He hadn't even noticed my new dress. While he made notes from my journal, I got my uniform ready for the morning. A couple of times he exclaimed with surprise.

When he finished, he looked up. "Good work, Anne. Where are the photos you took? I'd like to see them."

"I gave them to Dr. Chown."

"Negatives?"

"Oh, I have those. They're in an envelope in the back of the journal."

He flipped over the pages, drew out the envelope and held a strip of negatives up to the light. "What's this first one?"

I stepped over to the desk and explained the negatives. Michael kept nodding, interested.

"What a story," he said, leaning back with his hands behind his head. "I'd like to use the negatives."

"I don't know. I'd have to check with Dr. Chown. He's already in so much trouble, I'd hate to cause him any more."

"I understand," he said.

Then, for the first time since he had arrived, he seemed to really look at me. "Hey, you been to a party or something? You look terrific."

I smoothed my dress over my hips, pleased.

"All grown up," he smiled. "I'm tempted to stay, but I don't have time."

He went to the door and opened it cautiously. He was gone before I could say goodbye.

I don't know what made me open my journal before I replaced it under my mattress, but I did. The negatives were gone.

CHAPTER ELEVEN

I didn't sleep well. Memories of Michael kept stirring around. When I thought back, I saw he'd never been the person I imagined—hoped—he was. I was overcome by a feeling of dread, of terror, that Dr. Chown's investigation might be compromised because of this. It was the worst thing that had ever happened in my entire life. And to think I'd set it up by trying to help Michael with his newspaper story! Even my stomach was in an uproar.

In the morning as I dressed, my hands trembled as I buttoned my uniform. When I bent to tie my shoelaces, I thought my head would split open. I took a couple of Tylenol and went to meet Dr. Chown.

He and Mr. MacGregor, the public health engineer, who looked as dour as ever, came up the gangway. "The first thing is a trip to the number seven water tanks," Dr. Chown said. "They should be pumped almost dry by now. I'll take a sample from them for the meeting with the shipping line later this morning."

The three of us went down to the engine room, and Dr.

Chown asked that the hatches be removed. As he squeezed his stocky body through one hatch, I thought how much I admired him and everything he stood for. In contrast, Michael's action the evening before was despicable.

Should I tell Dr. Chown about Michael and the missing negatives? He had the right to know. I decided that I would tell him, the first chance I had. God, I thought, I hope my headache goes away before then—I can hardly think straight.

Dr. Chown came out holding a glass vial full of a muddy sludge. "I took it from the bottom of one of the tanks. There's about an inch of brown sediment that has settled there since we anchored last evening."

Mr. MacGregor took the vial from Dr. Chown, removed the stopper and held it to his nose. "I'm convinced," he said. "There's no doubt whatsoever. This is contaminated."

We were back at the hospital by the time the breakfast trays had been cleared away. Sister B. had traded shifts with the evening sister, and the hospital seemed calmer and quieter without Sister B. bustling about. We had fewer patients, too.

"I think we're over the worst," the sister said. "Other than Mrs. Kay. She's to be transferred to the city hospital at nine this morning."

At noon, Dr. Chown returned from the meeting with the World Wide Shipping representatives, and he called for Dr. Smythe and Dr. Connor to meet him in the midships hospital. I found something to do within hearing distance of the three men.

"I met with the shipping officials," Dr. Chown said. "Mr.

Hawkins, who flew in from London for the meeting, set the tone. He said, 'I've drunk a lot of so-called dirty water in my time, and I've never got sick.' So I pulled out the sample from my jacket pocket, placed it on the table before him and said, 'Well, try this.'" He paused briefly for effect. "Hawkins declined."

Dr. Smythe looked severe. Dr. Connor seemed not to be paying attention. I could hardly keep from applauding.

"I asked for an official report of the Southampton incident," Dr. Chown went on. "Hawkins read it out to me, and it sounded like a lawyer had written it. 'A minor spillage had taken place in Southampton.' Hawkins refused to hand over the report to me. He said, 'You can remember it. You're obviously an intelligent man.'"

"Did they say anything about chartering the Quantas jet?" asked Dr. Smythe. "The Australian and New Zealand passengers are anxious to get home."

"The company asked me what criteria they had to meet so that the passengers would be accepted back in their countries. I rattled off the details. They said, 'Wait a minute, wait a minute. We want to get this down.' So I said to them, 'No, you can remember it,' and I got up to leave."

Silently I cheered for Dr. Chown. "So now," he went on, "Hawkins hands me a copy of the report on Southampton. I go back to my seat and slowly repeat the list of criteria for them."

I grinned, proud of how Dr. Chown had handled it, and my face cracked with pain. My headache had returned tenfold, and I was hot.

I went to the utility room and took my temperature. A hundred and two. I panicked and went looking for one of the doctors. I caught up to Dr. Connor as he was pushing open the door on his way out of the hospital.

He examined me in the treatment room. "How long have you had this rash?" he asked.

"What rash?" I craned my neck to see where he'd found it.

"The one on your abdomen."

"I hadn't noticed anything before."

He pressed his hands hard into the left side of my abdomen, below my rib cage. "Does this hurt?"

"No."

"Constipated? Diarrhea?"

"Cramps."

"Headache?"

"Yes. Sort of ache all over."

"Tired?"

"That, too."

"We'll get you started on antibiotics."

I could hardly put the question into words. "You think it's typhoid?"

"We can't take a chance. We'll do some blood work right away, before we start the antibiotic. We'll want a stool culture, too. I'll send Sister in to admit you to the ship's hospital."

I tried to think back. I'd been so careful! How could I have picked up the typhoid bug? An image floated back into my mind: Bob Miller handing me a glass of ice water during my first meal on-board the *Ocean Spirit*. Saturday, January 10.

Nine days—within the incubation time, and not enough time for the vaccination that Dr. Connor had given me to work.

After Sister had admitted me to one of the beds and taken a blood sample, I tried to imagine what would happen to me now. How long would I likely be sick? And then what? I couldn't think clearly—until Sister came in with the antibiotic. It was not the half-grey, half-white Chloramphenicol capsule, but half-black, half-white—Tetracycline.

I palmed the pill and drank the water. For the first time, I missed Sister B. She wouldn't have let Dr. Connor order this less effective antibiotic. Ever since Henry Dixon had spoken to her, all patients with suspected typhoid received Chloramphenicol.

Tracey's face appeared at the door. "Tough luck, mate!" she said. "Anything I can do for you?"

"I need to see Mr. Dixon right away," I said. "Would you tell him, please?"

It couldn't have been more than five minutes before Henry Dixon stood at my bedside. I held out the capsule to him. I didn't have to say a word.

The next thing I knew, Sister was handing me four grey-and-white capsules of Chloramphenicol. I swallowed them gratefully.

"You did right to call me," Henry said. But I wondered what he would think if he knew that Michael had stolen the negatives, and that it was my fault.

He was quick to notice my change of expression, but misinterpreted it. "Don't take on, lass. You're getting a thousand milligrams—a gram—to get your blood level up in a hurry."

"Ta, luv," I said to him, feeling like the biggest traitor on earth.

Dr. Chown drove me to the Vancouver General in his own car. My body burned with fever and my head thudded. I'd taken my own pulse, and it was slow and full, just like the typhoid patients I'd taken care of.

"We haven't been able to prove that the Goanese steward is the carrier," said Dr. Chown as we waited for a traffic light to change. "He appears to be disgustingly healthy. I'll need a second blood test, but most of the Goanese will refuse to have them."

"Get Mr. Dixon to do them. He has a way with people." Listen to me talk—*traitor, traitor*—as if everything is okay between Dr. Chown and me, as if that bastard Michael didn't have the negatives, Dr. Chown's negatives, Dr. Chown, my hero.

"It's their culture, probably has to do with their religion."

The light changed and he accelerated. Even this gentle forward movement almost caused me to cry out with pain as my neck jerked.

A few blocks from the hospital, Dr. Chown cleared his throat. "I'm going to have to tell your parents, Anne, you know. About your illness."

"Not yet," I begged. "I could make a miraculous recovery. Besides, you don't know that it's typhoid. They've only just done the blood work." Every word hurt as I pulled it out of a mind that kept going in and out of focus.

"A day. I'll wait a day and no longer."

My joints ached, and I stretched out my legs to get some

relief. A chill came over me and my teeth began to chatter.

Dr. Chown parked in the physicians' lot, got me into a wheelchair and punched the elevator button. As it began to creak its way down, a newspaper box nearby caught Dr. Chown's eye. He fished for coins, bought the paper and looked at me with the face of a betrayed child.

"What's this all about?" he said, dropping the newspaper in my lap. With blurry eyes, I read the headline: *SS TYPHOID.* Below it was a familiar photo of a junior officer holding his hand at mid-thigh level. I choked with shame and dropped my head. I wanted to die.

In halting sentences, my head throbbing, I told him what had happened. His face looked like stone, his eyes unblinking. "I'm so sorry," I said finally, my voice breaking. "I really was going to tell you."

Finally his face softened. "It's not the end of the world," he said. "Besides, we've got our evidence now. Case closed." He actually smiled at me.

Relief flooded through me like a burst of sunlight after a terrifying storm. I couldn't speak, I was so choked with gratitude.

The elevator arrived, and soon I lay in a high hospital bed with a thermometer under my tongue and a blood pressure cuff wrapped around my upper arm.

"I'm going to leave you now, Anne," said Dr. Chown. "But I'll be back to see you at the end of my day. MacGregor and I are having all the ship's water tanks emptied and cleaned."

"I miss being part of the excitement."

"I know. You've been a great help to me, Anne. MacGregor's suggested putting a dye tracer, like fluorescein, into the sewage system to see if it turns up in the fresh-water supply."

"Henry Dixon has fluorescein," I managed to drag up from my memory. "He uses it to make up eye drops."

"I'll talk to him. It needs to be done. People are still getting sick. I'm sorry you had to be one of them." He squeezed my hand.

After Dr. Chown left, the enormity of being alone struck me. The room was bare as a cell, no drapes at the window, no picture on the wall. Outside, bare-limbed trees were etched against a purple sky. It must be late afternoon, I thought, close to dusk. A dry mouth, bowel cramps. A hurried trip to the bathroom and then another and another.

A different nurse came in response to my call light. Her cap askew untidy hair, shoes unpolished. Sister B. would have chewed her out for what she would call her "slovenly appearance." But she was gentle as she washed my back and rubbed it with lotion. She changed my gown and brought me apple juice. Then she sat and told me hospital stories until I thought I might live after all.

When Dr. Chown came in around midnight, I'd had two more doses of antibiotic and was able to tell him, "Yes, you can phone my parents. But I don't want them to visit me until I'm feeling a little better."

He seemed to accept that.

It was a long, miserable night. Sweats and linen changes and more sweats as my temperature dropped. I got so dehydrated, they had to start an IV.

By the time the sun rose, tinting the windows a rosy pink, I knew one thing. I wanted to see my mother.

CHAPTER TWELVE

The following days passed in a blur of tepid sponge baths to bring down my temperature when it soared, changes of linen and bottles of IV fluids hanging from a pole. An "In and Out" chart hung at the foot of my bed, and every drop I drank or passed was measured and recorded. An endless stream of interns, residents and student nurses came and went. They all asked the same questions and prodded the same spot under my left ribs. "Sometimes the spleen can be enlarged," one explained.

Bob Miller, who had come to see me the evening I was admitted and several times since, told me to refuse any further examinations or questions. "Just because it's a teaching hospital doesn't mean you can't tell them to leave you alone."

"In a way, it's comforting," I said. "At least someone cares. Oh, I don't mean you!" I added quickly. "I'm so glad you come to see me."

"How about your family? Why aren't they here?"

"Dr. Chown's in touch with them every day by phone. They'll come soon."

I missed my mother. I couldn't explain why, since I'd been so anxious to get away from her. Once, half-asleep, I'd seen her pull up my blanket that had slipped to the floor.

Now it was Bob who straightened the blanket on my bed. "Two new cases came in off the ship this morning," he told me. "But I heard one of the doctors say he thought the epidemic was over."

"How long does it take?" I fretted. "I need to get back to school. I don't want to lose the whole year."

"It can take three weeks. That's what my doc told me. But everyone's different."

"At least my red spots have disappeared. Bob, did you know that Captain Bunyon finally told Dr. Chown about the Southampton spill?"

"Good," Bob said, his face expressionless. "Not my place to say anything."

I wanted to blurt out, "But it was! It was!" But he had his own way of looking at things, and I was grateful that he was there for me now.

Dr. Chown came to visit almost every day. Sometimes it was as early as six in the morning, other times as late as midnight. I was always glad to see him.

I lost count of the days. It must have been about my fifth day in hospital when Dr. Chown said, "Your father will be here tomorrow."

"Not Mom?"

"Not for a while."

"Why?"

"Your father didn't say. I told him you were up to having visitors. Your temperature's still high, but that's not unusual. How are you feeling?"

"Sometimes I feel so drowsy, everything seems to shut down."

"That's toxicity, from the infection. It will pass."

"How's everyone on the ship?"

"They all ask about you, especially the third mate. Oh, that reminds me, I have a couple of letters for you."

One was from Tracey, the other from Dennis. I put them under my pillow.

Dr. Chown settled himself in the room's only chair, an uncomfortable wooden one with arms. "MacGregor has worked up a twenty-five-page formula for cleaning and purifying the ship's water tanks. All accessible water tanks are to be drained, scrubbed out with a near-lethal chlorine bleach solution and then refilled with massive chlorine-content water."

"I miss everything about the ship," I said.

Dr. Chown loosened his tie, leaned back and closed his eyes. The area under his eyes looked bruised and puffy. Even his voice sounded tired. "Not to worry, I'll keep you posted. After twenty-four hours, we'll empty, rinse, refill the tanks with fresh water and test for coliform."

"At least you know the source of the contamination," I said.

"It's taking much longer than we thought. The shipping company is putting a hell of a lot of pressure on me. They want the ship to sail."

I murmured a sound of sympathy.

"And there's a longshoremen's strike looming. If we don't

get the ship cleared and sailing, it could be tied up for months." He roused himself. "Enough of gloom. I have a bit of good news, Anne. The fluorescein we used to test for cross-contamination? None showed with the ultraviolet light."

As soon as Dr. Chown left, I read my letters. "Dear Anne," Tracey wrote. "Sorry you're sick, but maybe you'll meet some cute resident at the hospital and never want to come back. Get better soon. Tracey XXXOOO."

I opened the letter from Dennis.

Dearest Anne,

When they told me you were taken to hospital, it was all I could do not to leave the ship and go to you. If wishes come true, then you'll be better very soon. Take care of yourself.

All my love,

Dennis

The next afternoon, I heard the voices of Dr. Chown and my father coming down the hall toward my room. I sat up in bed eagerly.

Dad looked thinner than I remembered. Guilt flooded me, and I started to tremble.

"Oh, Anne!" said my father, hugging me. "You had us all so worried." He lifted his glasses and wiped his eyes with his handkerchief.

"I'll leave you two alone for a while," said Dr. Chown.

Dad sat in the armchair and drummed his fingers on the scarred wood. He cleared his throat several times, but didn't say anything.

"How's Mom?" I asked in a small voice.

"She isn't up to visiting you yet. Perhaps next week."

"Is she sick or something? She won't get typhoid from me, if that's what you're worried about."

"I know. By the way, I have a letter here for you, postmarked Panama. It must be your friend Judy."

And so it went—small talk that left everything important unsaid. I was relieved when Dr. Chown came back about fifteen minutes later, carrying another chair. I lay back in bed exhausted, closed my eyes and let the talk between Dad and Dr. Chown spill around me.

"Andy, I could lose my job over this," Dr. Chown said. "The company faces millions of dollars in lawsuits. I think the Canadian government wants to play it safe because they don't want to lose the revenue from a major port of call."

"What do they want you to do?"

"Soft-pedal it. As a scientist, you know I can't do that."

"I doubt the government wants facts," Dad agreed. "What they want is to avoid any problems."

Silence for a moment.

Dad again. "Were you ever able to isolate the carrier?"

"Carriers, plural. Two, possibly three. We had to wait to get a virulence antigen from London. There was none here in Canada. Once we had that, we tested our prime suspect. This Goanese steward has been healthy throughout, but he showed a very high positive response to the antigen. He's still excreting typhoid bacilli in his stool."

"The other two carriers?" Dad asked.

"Two other crewmen who had moderate responses. They're

still excreting bacilli, too. But the chief carrier is the Goanese steward. We're not naming him, of course. It would be devastating for him." Dr. Chown cleared his throat. "Needless to say, he is banned from handling any food or drink."

"I read in the paper that he'd been treated as a typhoid suspect in a South Africa hospital and that all tests were negative," Dad said. The more he talked with Dr. Chown, the more real he seemed to become—more like the dad I'd known.

Dr. Chown slapped his thigh for emphasis. "This man *must* have had typhoid in Cape Town. He had to have been released without being treated so he is still a carrier."

"Of course, that's my wife's big concern—that Anne could be a carrier."

Dr. Chown stood up and put his hand on Dad's shoulder. "Only two to five percent become carriers, and that's because they weren't treated. Your wife has nothing to worry about with Anne."

I slid way down in bed, wanting to disappear.

Their talk turned to their student days at university. "Are you still working on Co-enzyme A?" Dr. Chown asked Dad.

"I had a couple of papers published. But once you get married and have a family, you realize that basic research is too demanding."

"Pity," said Dr. Chown, his face neutral. "Your work was brilliant."

I tried to read Dad's face. Regret? No. Resignation.

By the end of the second week, my temperature had begun to stay down. "Your blood and stool cultures are positive now for typhoid bacillus," Dr. Chown told me. "So is your urine, and your serum agglutination."

"What does that mean?"

"That your body is putting up a fight. Next week you can expect your temperature to return to normal. We'll keep testing the stools until they are negative."

"My mom still hasn't come." I tried not to sound the way I felt—abandoned.

"I understand illness of any kind upsets your mother."

"Everything upsets her." Every time I thought about my mother, sadness welled up in my throat and threatened to choke me. I changed the subject. "What's the latest on-board ship?"

"Well, I have your usual letter from Dennis Wilson." He reached into the inner pocket of his jacket. "As for news, let's see. Some of the passengers have been cleared medically and have flown back to New Zealand or Australia."

"Did you ever get all of the water tanks cleaned out?"

"Finally, although we had a problem with one of them. We tried three times, and it was still dirty. So MacGregor and the chief officer put on overalls and scrubbed it out themselves. MacGregor complains that he ruined his shoes doing it."

"But now he's satisfied it's clean?"

"Not quite. He cut out sections of pipe—even Captain Bunyon's bathroom wasn't exempt. MacGregor thought the pipes could be so corroded, or contain so much organic material, the chlorine in the water would be used up before reaching the taps."

"I heard you tell Dad that you could lose your job. Was it

because of Michael's article and pictures in the newspaper? I feel so terrible about that!"

"Don't give it another thought, Anne. I have been threatened, blackmailed and coerced from the very beginning by Ottawa. They've even held a kangaroo court. And that was long before any article or photo appeared in the press."

"I read in the *Sun* that Captain Bunyon says there are fourteen and a half miles of fresh-water plumbing on the ship and that no typhoid bacteria were ever found."

Dr. Chown shrugged his shoulders. "Easy to put a spin on the facts to suit the occasion."

In the middle of the third week my temperature dropped to normal, and I felt much better. Until a visit from Nana.

She wore a tailored navy blue suit with a frilly white blouse that did nothing to soften the hard line of her jaw. "I'm exceedingly disappointed in you, Anne," she said as soon as she was in my room.

My gut flipped in protest.

"The worry you've caused your family is unforgivable," she continued. "Your poor mother!"

"Mom hasn't been to visit me yet," I said, unable to keep the disappointment and anger out of my voice.

"What do you expect? Do you have any idea of the grief you've caused her?"

I got out of bed and began walking back and forth like a bear in a cage.

"What are you planning to do when you're discharged?" Nana asked.

I stopped my pacing and turned to her in surprise. "Go home, of course."

"Your parents and I have been talking it over," Nana said carefully. "This might be the time for you to come over to Victoria and be a boarder at my school. You'll have a private room, but of course there will be no special privileges for you."

"Do you have a strong science program?"

"If that isn't typical, Anne! We meet the high school curriculum, and that is quite good enough. What is far more important is that you would learn to be a lady."

It didn't pay to argue with Nana. I let it drop.

But after she left, I walked down the hall to the phone and dialed Aunt Ruth's number. When I heard her cheery voice, I almost sank to my knees with thankfulness. I couldn't keep the tears from my voice when I told her where I was and why.

"Are you allowed visitors?" she said.

"Yes."

"I'll be there in an hour."

Feeling immensely cheered, I went back to my room, shampooed my hair and put on lipstick. I was waiting by the elevator when Aunt Ruth burst forth in a cloud of violet perfume and a swirl of her long red coat. Her fingernails were enamelled to match. It was as though I had moved into sunlight after being too long in a cold shadow.

"I've brought you a couple of books I know you'll love and your favourite jelly beans," she said. "And just wait 'til you hear about my trip!"

CHAPTER THIRTEEN

Bob Miller dropped into my room to say goodbye. "I've been discharged," he said. "I can go back to the ship—just in the nick of time, too. She'll be sailing any day now."

"That's wonderful, Bob, I'm so glad. Dr. Chown's going to take me down before she leaves so that I can say goodbye to everyone."

"We'll be back in about four months, the seventh of June, I think. Would you like to go out for dinner with me?"

"Sounds great!" I still wasn't sure about Bob. Shouldn't he have reported the sloppy cleanup at Southampton so that something could be done? But perhaps he did. Or maybe there was no way of knowing that it had flooded over the No. 7 water tanks. I didn't know.

But what I did know is that I'd spent many sleepless nights in the hospital, and it had given me time to think. Like about heroes. What they were and what they weren't. Michael had been my hero when I was a child. He knew how to fix bikes and be kind to small, pesky girls. But now, after what he did …

Bob's words broke into my thoughts. "Will you be living

in San Francisco, or in Vancouver?"

"I live near San Francisco. My parents are supposed to be here by the end of the week to take me home."

"Can I have your address?"

As I wrote it down, I was surprised by the negative emotions that came swirling up at the thought of home. I could see myself back there with my mother, who would be shocked and furious if I dared say what I thought. I'd have to tiptoe around all her stated and unstated rules. I could already hear Dad's voice saying, "You are not to upset your mother." Dad, once my biggest hero.

Dr. Chown came to pick me up in his own car. "Are you excited about going back to the ship?" he asked.

"Oh, yes. And glad to be better and out of the hospital."

The traffic was light on Broadway, and I leaned back, enjoying my return to a world that had moved closer to springtime. The February sun made the sky even bluer.

As we approached the CPR dock, I caught sight of the *Ocean Spirit*, and I stopped breathing for a moment. I had forgotten how graceful and beautiful the ship was, and how much I had come to love her. The Blue Peter flag on the foremast signalled that she was under sailing orders.

Because it was departure day, there was a mob scene, and Dr. Chown had trouble manoeuvring the car to his usual parking spot. Delivery vans, produce trucks and taxis jammed the dock. Winches squealed, horns honked, longshoremen yelled. A long line of utility stewards were working stores on a chain gang, passing boxes of BC canned salmon unloaded from a truck up the gangway and into the ship through an open galley gunport.

After we parked the car, we had to dodge and dart, push and shove to get to the gangway. I recognized a few of the people boarding as VIPs whose faces I'd seen on magazine covers.

"I want to stop at the deucer's office to pick up my paycheque," I told Dr. Chown.

"We'll meet back at the car in about an hour," he said.

The ship was crowded with passengers and visitors, and everywhere there was the smell of flowers, perfume and liquor. Excited conversation and bursts of laughter nearly drowned out the music playing over the PA system. Every few minutes, someone was paged.

I had to push my way past the lineup at Cece Rathbone's office. He glanced up from his desk when I spoke his name. "Oh, it's you," he grunted.

"I've come for my paycheque."

"I can't attend to it now. Far too busy. We'll have to mail it to you."

To the fake address? "No," I said. "I need it now." My knees were trembling so badly, I had to clench them together to control them.

But after a moment, Cece gave in. "I think I may have the cheque here in the drawer," he said.

I opened the sealed envelope he handed me and looked at the figure on the cheque. Sixty-six pounds minus thirteen pounds and sixteen shillings for uniforms from the slop chest. I calculated quickly: roughly 173 dollars.

"Thanks, sweetheart," I muttered as I went out the door.

I headed to the dispensary to see Henry Dixon, passing the midships hospital on my way. Sister B. came through the door, and when she saw me, she smiled. The sight stopped me dead in my tracks.

"I'm glad you're better," she said. And while I was still reeling from that, she added, "I want you to know I think you have the makings of an excellent nurse. That is, if you put your mind to it."

I managed to blurt out my thanks. Tracey had told me once that she heard Sister call me "a regular little madam," which I had taken (correctly, as Henry Dixon later confirmed) to be derogatory. Wait 'til I told Tracey about this.

I found Henry Dixon restocking the shelves. "You're a bright sight," he said. "I kept tabs on you while you were in the hospital, so I knew you were getting better. We had a total of fifty-four crewmen and eleven passengers come down with typhoid. It will go down in medical history."

"At least no one died."

"There was one death, Anne. Mr. Haywood, that sixty-four-year-old passenger from Australia. He died of complications—staphylococcal pneumonia."

"I remember him," I said, shaken. "He was my patient the first day I worked in the hospital."

"Well, lass …"

"I've come to say goodbye, Mr. Dixon. I'm going back to school."

"Back to live with your mum, then?"

I gulped. After a moment, he said, "You've learned a fair bit this trip, haven't you?"

"Yes. And I'll never forget you, Mr. Dixon." I hated it when I couldn't hold back tears. I wanted to tell him that I thought he was a hero, too. But I couldn't find the right words. Smart, kind, but more than that. He cared about his job, he cared about people.

"Now then, don't go soft on me, luv. You'll do great things with your life, and if you ever get to Tassie, come and have a cuppa with the missus and me. The door's always open."

"Ta, luv, Mr. Dixon."

I bumped into Tracey soon after I left the dispensary. She was carrying a baby, and two toddlers hung onto her skirt. "Help!" she said. "The nursery is filling up with screaming kids. Stay and give us a hand."

"As if I could! Love to, though. Will I see you again?"

"Perhaps. You could always write."

"I will. Know where I could find Dennis?"

"Right behind you, mate."

I whirled, and there he was.

"I saw you come up the gangway when you boarded with Dr. Chown," he said. "But I couldn't leave the wheelhouse. As it is, I've only got a few minutes. Come up top with me."

I followed him to the boat deck, and he led me to a secluded space behind a lifeboat. I had a quick, unwelcome thought: had he taken other females to this same spot? "I have something for you," he said, taking a gold ring off his little finger. "It belonged to my grandmother. I wear it for luck." He reached for my left hand.

I pulled back. "Dennis, I—"

"A friendship ring, Anne."

"Friends ... all right, then. I'd like that."

We exchanged addresses, and he took his time kissing me. It was more than a friendly kiss.

I stood and watched him walk into the wheelhouse, and I was still there a few minutes later when Captain Bunyon and Dr. Chown come out of the door. I moved closer as Dr. Chown handed the captain a piece of paper. It must be the certificate that said the ship's water was pure.

Moments later, the two yellow quarantine flags came plummeting down. At the same time, a boys' band on the dock played the opening bars of "Anchors Aweigh."

Passengers began unfurling an enormous banner to hang over the side of the ship. It was four feet high and reached from the bow to the stern. From where I stood, I could see that it had bright red letters, but I couldn't make them out. Hundreds of streamers began to fly through the air, like brightly coloured ribbons tying the ship to the dock.

I made my way to the gangway to disembark and met Sister B. again. This time she wore her blue nurse's cape and had her arms full of presents, which the passengers were piling into her arms.

Back on the dock I watched the city's medical staff walk down the gangway, looking exhausted but triumphant.

"Do you have a statement, sir?" a familiar voice asked. It was Michael. "Would it be fair to say that the *Ocean Spirit* is no longer a 'plague ship,' a 'floating time bomb'?"

"We don't know if any of the passengers are incubating the disease at the present time," answered one of the city officials. "But we do know that there will be no further infections from contaminated drinking water. We are well satisfied that the epidemic has been contained."

I dropped back into the crowd and made my way to Dr. Chown's car. From there I could read the red letters on the banner over the side of the ship: "Thank You! VANCOUVER." The band began to play "Will Ye No Come Back Again?"

As tugs edged the ship slowly away from the CPR wharf, a tremendous cheer went up from the passengers and crowd on the dock. I cheered, too, although my face was wet with tears.

CHAPTER FOURTEEN

I was writing a letter when Dr. Chown came into my hospital room. Right behind him came one of the aides with my afternoon snack.

"You're in the clear, Anne," he said. "There are no signs of you being a carrier. You know that you can't work in the food industry, of course."

"I wasn't planning to. But do you think I'm a menace if I prepare any food, anywhere?"

"You can cook at home, but you must be scrupulous about washing your hands after using the washroom."

"I already do!" After Sister B., I thought of myself as an expert on hand-washing.

"And, of course, wash your hands before you handle any food," he continued. "For example, right now, before you reach for that cookie."

I came back from the bathroom suitably chagrined. "Does that mean I'm discharged?"

"Yes. I'll phone your parents and let them know."

"I can do that," I said quickly.

"You'll need to see your family doctor when you get back home. You will have to be tested at six months and again at twelve months."

"I thought I'd go to my Aunt Ruth's for a day or so. I'll phone my parents from there."

He nodded. "Okay, get your things together, and we'll get you signed out. I'll drive you to your aunt's."

As he drove, Dr. Chown's mouth was set in an angry straight line. He must have felt me watching him because his eyes flicked quickly to mine.

I shifted uneasily in the seat. What was troubling him, now that the epidemic was over and the cover-up had been exposed? I didn't feel I had the right to ask. The late afternoon sun had dropped to the southern horizon and shone directly into our eyes. Dr. Chown put on his sunglasses.

"Aunt Ruth has invited you to dinner," I said, after a few minutes.

"Oh, I don't know—"

"She's a gourmet cook. She said to tell you she has a filet mignon and a bottle of Bordeaux red to celebrate."

"I guess I can't say no to that."

After dinner, I had to excuse myself. "I've got to go to bed. I can't keep my eyes open." Since I'd been sick, I'd often slept for twelve hours straight.

I lay in Aunt Ruth's guest room and listened to her and Dr. Chown talking in the living room. Their voices were a pleasant murmur, and I was drifting off to sleep when I heard my name spoken by Dr. Chown and woke up in an instant.

"I've felt an empathy for Anne ever since I met her," he said, "though I couldn't quite understand what was going on at home to make her bolt like that."

"You'd have to meet my sister, and even then it would take you a while to believe it. She can wear you down until you either give in, or you run for your life."

"Give me an example."

I was listening closely now.

"Well, for instance, she's been hell bent on sending Anne to boarding school. Anne refused, of course. So my dear sister arranged for Nana to take her there after Christmas break. I don't know how Anne found out about it. All she was told was that Nana was coming while they were away in Hawaii. Intuition, I guess. Anyway, that's when she bolted."

"Anne's too independent for boarding school," said Dr. Chown. "With the right kind of encouragement, there's no telling how far she'll go. The sky's the limit for that girl."

"You and I think so. But not my sister. All she sees when she looks at Anne is someone who has a mind of her own."

There was a silence. I heard the fireplace screen being moved, the thud of a piece of firewood, and then the crackling and snapping of pitch igniting. Aunt Ruth must not realize that I could hear every word they said.

"Power and control," said Dr. Chown. "I'm running into it myself. The federal government says they've lost confidence in me, that I lack discretion. They're wanting to get rid of me."

"Surely not! After the magnificent job you did containing the typhoid epidemic?"

"I can fight them legally, of course. An MP has already

raised the question in the House of Commons. But they have ways of dealing with people who don't comply. They'll move me sideways into what is essentially a demotion. Maybe that's what I like about Anne. She has an original mind and dares to ask questions and think for herself."

"That is exactly what my sister can't stand."

"You're not like your sister."

"No, I'm ten years older and more like my father. I look like him and act like him. Something *my* mother couldn't stand, since he dared join up at the start of the war and got himself killed."

"And round and round it goes in families, doesn't it? Still, I'm seriously considering quitting the government job and beating them to it. I could go into private practice. I'd like to get married and have a family." I heard the clink of crystal.

"Why don't you, if that's what you want?" Too bad Aunt Ruth was too old for Dr. Chown.

"What I *want* more is to have my name cleared and get some recognition for the job I've done." A chair was pushed back.

Aunt Ruth spoke. "Maybe that won't happen, and maybe you'll have to live with it." Her voice was kind but practical and reminded me of when I'd fall down skiing, and she'd say, "Get up and try again."

Silence again, and then, with a softened voice, she said, "If you could turn the clock back a month and do it all over again, would you do anything different?"

"No, I couldn't. I never dreamed it would be this painful to be honest, but I did what I had to do, the best way I knew."

"No one can do more than that," she said with conviction. "Let's drink to that and your future. And as my dear departed father used to say, 'Screw the bastards.'"

I fell asleep thinking about Dr. Chown and the choices he'd made and the ones he had yet to make. One thing I knew: he was my biggest hero of all.

It took me until sunset the next day to call home. I took the phone over to the couch by the window, where the boulevard trees showed black against the golden glow of the sunset. My mother answered in her soft, breathless voice.

"Mom? This is Anne." I couldn't keep the tremor out of my voice, and I began shaking.

"Anne! Are you phoning from the hospital?"

"No, Aunt Ruth's. I've been here a couple of days."

"I'll call your father."

"No, I have something to tell you." I took a deep breath and stood up straight. "I'm not coming home."

"Andrew!" she called, her hand not quite covering the mouthpiece. "Come quickly! It's Anne, and she's being difficult again. I will *not* deal with her when she's like this."

"Anne?" Dad's voice.

"I'm not going home. I'm going to stay with Aunt Ruth and go to school here."

His breathing turned ragged. "Your mother will never allow it. You know how she feels about the way your aunt lives. If you love your mother, you'll come home immediately."

"I can't, Dad."

"Be reasonable, Anne. Look at the mess you're in now by being stubborn."

"You mean the typhoid? I've recovered. I'm not a carrier."

"What are you going to do for money? Your aunt spends all she has on clothes and travelling, and I'm not going to support you to do something that upsets your mother."

"I've got a part-time job lined up at the Vancouver General Hospital. I start next weekend working as a clerk in their admitting department."

I could hear my mother having hysterics in the background. Poor Dad. But why did he put up with it and take her side? "Maybe at the end of the term, I could come home for a visit," I said. "We could talk about it again."

"You are a terrible, terrible disappointment to your mother."

"I'm sorry, Dad. But I've made up my mind."

Now he sounded bewildered and plaintive. "I don't know what I'm going to say to her."

"What I'm doing is really not that bad. Tell Mom that."

I enrolled at Kitsilano High School the next day. I found I had a lot of reading to do to catch up in English, but I was ahead in science and math. I joined the Science Club and started planning my project—a full report on the typhoid epidemic.

One day I ran into Michael Smith. I'd gone to the White Spot after school, and there he was, sitting at one of the tables, a hamburger and strawberry shake before him.

After we exchanged hellos, I said, "I thought you were

going to Nelson to live in one of the communes."

"No, I'm working for the *Province*. That exposé I did on the *Ocean Spirit* opened a lot of doors for me."

I began to move away before I said something I'd regret. He stopped me. "Would you like to go to a concert with me this weekend?" he asked. "Local talent, but not bad."

"Thanks, but I'm going with someone right now."

I wasn't, but there was this brain who was my partner in the science lab, and we got along really well. Who knew what might happen?

In the meantime, the *Ocean Spirit* was due in Vancouver in a couple of weeks, and I would be seeing Dennis. Dr. Chown planned to leave for Ontario by the end of the month to start his family practice, and he'd be over for dinner at least a couple of more times before then.

I'd thought about Michael a lot. Maybe he was the way he was because he was a draft dodger and had to live by his wits. Maybe he was driven by ambition. Whatever the reason—compared to the people I'd met since I left home—he just didn't measure up.

No, I didn't have time for the Michaels of the world.

Dad. What to think about him? In spite of his threat, he'd begun to send Aunt Ruth money every month to pay my expenses.

He phoned me every week. The last time we spoke, I said, "I've decided I'm going to go into medicine."

"Since when?"

"It started when I was sick in the hospital, and it's been

growing ever since. Next year I'm going to take Latin and chemistry, and I'll check out the scholarships."

"UBC?"

"No, McGill. Like you and Dr. Chown."

He was silent for a moment.

"Well, Anne," he said at last. "I'll be proud to help you any way I can."

This work of fiction is based on a true incident. In the early 1970s, the Centres for Disease Control and Prevention (CDC) established the Vessel Sanitation Program (VSP) in co-operation with the cruise ship industry to insure the purity of all drinking water and the safe handling of sewage. There has not been a reported shipboard typhoid epidemic on a cruise ship since.